John Maclean

The Warden of the Plains

And Other Stories of Life in the Canadian Northwest

John Maclean

The Warden of the Plains
And Other Stories of Life in the Canadian Northwest

ISBN/EAN: 9783337190132

Printed in Europe, USA, Canada, Australia, Japan

Cover: Foto ©Andreas Hilbeck / pixelio.de

More available books at **www.hansebooks.com**

" Boys, I allus carries my Guide-Book."   (Page 5.)

THE WARDEN OF THE PLAINS

AND OTHER STORIES OF LIFE IN THE
CANADIAN NORTH-WEST

BY

JOHN MACLEAN, M.A., Ph.D.,

Author of " Canadian Savage Folk," etc.

ILLUSTRATED BY J. E. LAUGHLIN

TORONTO
WILLIAM BRIGGS
WESLEY BUILDINGS

MONTREAL: C. W. COATES   HALIFAX: S. F. HUESTIS
1896

CONTENTS.

THE WARDEN OF THE PLAINS.

O N the wide western plains at the base of the Rocky Mountains, where countless buffalo once found luxuriant feeding-grounds, the white man's cattle were roaming in tens of thousands. It was the time of the "round up." The cowboys had been scouring the plain for hundreds of miles gathering in the cattle and horses, banding them and driving them into the corral, there to be counted and the young branded.

The "round up" party had camped for the night. Many of them were weary from the hard day's riding, and were sitting or lounging about in the tents or on the open prairie, waiting for the supper which others were preparing.

"Hello, Jake!" shouted one of these, as a man who seemed to have sprung from the prairie, so suddenly had he appeared, rode into the camp.

"All right, Bill," was the reply of the new-comer, uttered in a short but friendly tone.

"The boys 'll be right glad t' see ye, Jake, fur we haven't had a sermon fur a long time. Ye're the only preacher we fellows have got, and ye're welcome."

"Wall, Bill, ef ye wud follow the trail and no be straying frae the herd, ye wouldna get lost sae often, nur make it sae hard fur yerselves, and fur the Gospel cowboys t' find ye."

Jake, or as he called himself, the "Gospel Cowboy," was a queer character but a true man, who felt himself called upon to go from ranch to ranch to tell in his own strange way the story of the Saviour's love.

Before his conversion he was known as "Broncho Jake," but since then the pioneers on the prairie had called him "The Warden of the Plains." He was a daring fellow, fearless of danger in crossing the rapid rivers, a good rider and a splendid roper. Few of the cowboys could handle a lariat like Broncho Jake. He was always foremost in trials of skill and horsemanship. A few years before he had entered upon his new life of itinerating among the ranches, there was a contest between the cowboys to decide who among them was the most skilful rider. Jake was one of the competitors.

A large circle was formed upon the prairie where the contest was to be held. The various riders were surrounded by friends who had come to witness the exhibition of skill. Many feats of daring were performed, until the contest lay finally between Bill Jones and Broncho Jake.

Bill sprang lightly upon his horse, and riding rapidly around the circle, flung his hat to the ground; then increasing the animal's speed until it became a mad rush through space, he leaned downward on the right side, and holding on only by his left foot, picked up the hat, and, putting it on his head, threw himself back into the saddle. The crowd cheered him lustily as he sat his horse with easy grace and rode once more around the circle. The horse seemed to understand and feel that his master's reputation was at stake, and his nostrils quivered as he stretched his neck forward in the race. Still riding at full speed, Bill loosed his necktie and threw it on the ground. Surely he does not mean to attempt to pick it up! If he tries he will certainly break his neck. Bill rode once more round the ring; then throwing the reins on the neck of the sure-footed animal, while every eye was strained to catch his slightest movement, he bent forward, and with a sudden dash as he rode past where it lay, he grasped the necktie in his fingers and lifted it from the ground, waving it in the air as he rode onward to the starting-place. The cowboys were delighted.   Many of them ran to him, seized his hands and expressed their hearty admiration of his skill.

It was then Jake's turn to show what he could do, and although everyone was interested, they felt that the contest was ended, and many of them said so.

"Bet yer life Jake can't beat that!"

Jake took no notice of this expression of public opinion, but threw himself on his horse as indifferently as if such contests were of everyday occurrence. Riding easily around the ring two or three times as if to get himself into trim for his work, he threw his hat on the ground, and as he rode past picked it up.   Taking off his necktie, he cast that on the prairie and picked it up as deftly as Bill had done.   The crowd were surprised.   They had not thought Jake capable of such a daring feat.   But he had not exhausted his ability to astonish them.   Riding around as before, Jake flung down both hat and tie, and as he passed them on his next round leaned forward and picked up first one and then the other with his teeth: then turning to the crowd, who were cheering him loudly, he waved his hand in acknowledgment of their praise, and rode quietly homeward.   Broncho Jake was henceforward honored by the boys.   When he joined the ranks of the "Gospel grinders" there were wry faces made and queer remarks uttered, for some of the boys thought he would be sentimental and sanctimonious: but there were others who knew him better and said, "Jake's a square fellow, and you bet he'll be a good un; none o' yer long faces nur yer long prayers when a fellow is in need of anything."

Jake justified his friends' faith, and no one exerted a wider influence for good over the cowboys, or was given a heartier welcome when he came among them, than "The Warden of the Plains."

On this evening as soon as supper was over, the boys gathered round Jake and were soon singing the hymns he had set to the rollicking airs all cowboys love.

Jake had a grand supply of stories, and when the lads were in good spirits they would listen eagerly, unconsciously learning the lesson the story never failed to convey. Jake was too wise to draw the moral of his tales himself, thus treating his audience as children. He told his stories in a fascinating and suggestive manner, and left each listener to adapt their teaching to his own need or consciousness.

Much, however, as they liked his stories, the great event of Jake's visit was his sermon. The boys loved to hear him preach. He talked to them in language and in a way that they could understand, and his genuine goodness of heart and interest in their welfare had taught them to love him. It was a rough kind of affection, and the boys would not have called it by that name, perhaps, but it was none the less a genuine love for the man.

Taking a little book out of his pocket, Jake looked around on the men who sat about him, and smiling as he held it up, said:

" Ye see, boys, I allus bring my brand Book wi' me to see to the strays and return them to the masters. I've got nearly all the brands by heart. The biggest cattle-bosses I've known—an' a good many I've met in my day—are the Lord Jesus Christ and the devil. I'm a wee bit afeard the devil's got the biggest herd, for his range is cropped off bare, and the cattle are pretty thin. He's no a bit partic'ler how he gets them, mavrocks, strays and sich like, he puts his brand on them all. Sich a lot of scrubs you never saw afore. Puir things, wi' a hummocky, stony range they get hardly anythin' to eat.

" I've ridden over the range, an' I reckon I know what it's like. His herd is just like Slim Jim's, where the cattle feed on furze and rushes, thinkin' they're fine grass and vetches, but ye can tell when ye see their ribs they're no well herded. I reckon the cowboys are asleep, an' the puir things maun rustle fur themselves. Ah, ma lads, ye're among the strays the devil has stolen, an' he's put his brand on ye. Ye canna see his mark, fur he's put it pretty well on yer flanks. He's a cunnin' cattle-boss. He's afeard the owner might claim ye, for would ye believe it, ye belong to the herd of Christ, an' ye've strayed, and some of ye were mavrocks. It's easy to get lost on the prairie when ye take the wrong trail, an' some of ye hae jist shut yer eyes an' followed the ithers ahead o' ye. I reckon the Christ cowboys and the devil's cowboys hae pretty hard times when they meet on the prairie. It's none o' yer wee fights, but a strong tussle. They're just like the big cattle-bosses I wus a readin' about that got into trouble about their ranges. There wus Old Abe and Parson Lot. Wall, they had big herds, an' they got cropped bare, an' one day Abe, the cattle-boss, looked out o' his ranch and he sees Parson Lot, the other big cattle-boss, a comin' wi' his cowboys an' cattle, an' they was a singin'

'We're comin', Father Abraham,
    Wi' three hundred thousand more.'

"Old Abe wasna pleased at Lot's puttin' on airs like that, and he says, 'Come in!' They sat down in the cattle-boss's shanty, and he says, 'See here, this is not going to do. If the cowboys get a fightin' the

Injuns an' half-breeds will come an' drive us out, so
ye see it wull pay us to be friends.' Lot turns to
him and says, 'That's what's the matter.'

"Wall, the two bosses rode over the country pro-
spectin', an' Abe says, 'It's a big country; make your
choice, Lot, fur I respec' ye, ye're an honest chap.'

"Wall, Lot went to the prairies o' the Jordan, an'
Abram went to the range o' Canaan. That ended
their wee bit spat. An' that's the way to settle
squabbles on the ranches. Jist separate them, an'
that will save powder, an' none o' the cowboys will
get scalped. If ye're no contented to herd for Lot, I
guess Abram would give ye a job, an' he pays well,
an' the grub is good.

"I tell ye, the devil's a good roper, an' his boys are
up to all kinds o' pranks. Get on his range an' he'll
hae ye coralled an' his mark on ye afore ye know it.
Christ is a fine boss, an' don't you forget it. His
cattle are all slick an' fat, an' his cowboys allus
engage again after their time's out. Stick to him,
my lads. He disna say much, but ye get the best o'
everything!"

Jake fell upon his knees and prayed briefly:

"Blessed Maister, we love you, an' we're not
ashamed to tell everybody. We oughter be ashamed
if we didna tell. Some of us are not on the right

trail. We've lost it, and we canna find it. The snow must o' covered it, or else our eyesight is gettin' bad an' we canna see. Corral us, O Lord, afore we get lost in the storm. Brand us wi' yer ain mark, that ye'll ken yer ain. Keep us on yer ain range, an' if ever we stampede, throw yer rope an' lead us to yer ranch. Save us frae wand'rin' in the mountains or strayin' in the coulees when there's fine feed on the prairie. Help us to feed on grace an' truth, an' may we be prepared to walk in the trails o' heaven; no runnin' an' tossin' up the horns, but walkin' an' lyin' down, sae peaceful like. When we're faint in the winter, an' there's no room fur us in the herd, or in the stables at the ranch, take us quietly some night, when there's nobody lookin', an' when we get hame we'll thank ye oursels fur all yer kindness an' love. Amen!"

Before sunrise the camp was astir, and Jake, bidding his friends good-bye, continued his journey after partaking of a hasty meal.

Few were the houses on the prairie, and frequently did this "sky pilot," as he was sometimes called, travel from forty to fifty miles to visit some aged miner or sick cowboy.

"An' yer lyin' there yet, Jim," said Jake, as he entered the shack of an old-timer who had been sick for a few weeks.

" Ay, Jake, it's hard lines, but I might be worse."

" That's true. Ye never looked on it that way afore, an' I'm glad to hear ye talk in that way."

Jake threw off his coat and stepped outside without saying a word, and in a few moments the vigorous play of an axe was heard. It was Jake putting in a preface to his sermon. Oftentimes he would say, " Ye maun heed the Book, fur it tells ye afore ye eat ye maun work, an' a clean religion is to creep down quietly afore anyone sees ye to the widow's house, an' split wood an' carry water. Ye min' that publican? I reckon he must hae been a cowboy when he was young. Afore he prayed he struck his breast pretty hard, an' then he prayed; but that Pharisee was too lazy an' proud, fur he prayed first. Now, ye maun work afore ye preach or pray or eat. Ye see it means if ye dinna work ye'll get so fat ye'll no be healthy, an' if ye don't take exercise prayin' a bit, readin' the Book awhile, choppin' wood fur the widows an' sheerin' sheep fur the orphans, ye'll be lazy an' unco clumsy. An' if ye get fat the devil will soon get ye, fur he's allus on the lookout fur fat cattle.

" The Maister didna think much o' them publicans, but I reckon He had a kind o' hankerin' after that un that cried, ' God be merciful!' "

"Publicans! I should think yer Master wouldn't travel on the same trail with them, fur they're the fellows as sells ye bad whiskey fur a big price, an' when yer dimes are gone, turn ye out on the prairie," said Jim.

"Ye're on the wrong trail, Jim; them publicans were Nor'-West lawyers, who charge ye thirty per cent. fur lendin' money, an' when ye borrow a hunner dollars gie ye sixty-four. I know them, fur I've been there. Some o' them fellers will hae to strike their breasts pretty hard afore the Maister 'll hear the crack."

Jake had a roaring fire on, and was soon busy making pancakes, buns and tea, and frying some bacon.

Jim was badly crippled with rheumatism, and seldom saw anyone except a cowboy or an Indian. He did not, however, feel lonely, as he had been accustomed to this mode of living for many years. The present year had been one of the hardest for him, he had suffered so much with rheumatism. Jim had been well brought up, his connections being numbered amongst some of the first families of Philadelphia. When quite a young man he had drifted westward, attracted by the report of the fortunes made at the mines. His life had been one of expectancy, always

hoping for the fortune which seemed to others a long
way off.   He was not daunted in his pursuit of
wealth.   Several times he had made large sums and
then squandered them freely, hoping to replace them
by greater; but that happy day never came to him,
and now he was almost a helpless cripple, crawling
around his shanty, and glad to see the face of
a stranger. There was none more welcome than
Broncho Jake. Jim had known him before he
became a "sky pilot," and so fully did he believe him,
that no one dared to say a word against him in his
hearing.

"The slap-jacks are no the best, Jim, but I reckon
they'll keep life in for a while."

"They're fine, Jake, they're fine."

"The Maister," said Jake, "must ha been a good
one, for He wus worse off than our rabbits; He didna
hae a hole to creep into out o' the sight o' His enemies:
an' min', He had a lot o' them, fur He was the friend
on the side o' the men who had their failings and had
none to sympathize with them.   When a cowboy
went off on the wrong trail an' got lost,—wi' drink, I
mean,—He wud come after him an' make signs like
the Indians, an' shout, 'Come back, ye're on the wrong
trail!'

"He didn't trample ye down when ye fell, but

waited till ye got yer breath, an' then takin' yer arm, He wud say, 'My friend, get up; ye'll soon be well. I'll gie ye a hand to put ye on yer horse, an' I'll help ye to find the trail.' He was a bonnie man, an' don't you forget it; none o' yer gentry, but a real man, wha, if He were here among us, wud dress in 'chapps' an' sombrero, an' ride a fine horse. I reckon He wud beat us a' at the ropin' an' ridin' an' sich like. I wud allus let Him beat me if I thought I could do better than Him."

Jim was silent. He had finished his meal and drawn near to the stove. He had seldom thought of such things until Jake began to visit him, and then his mind was directed towards religion, but in the quaint way which was characteristic of these men of the western plains. Jim sat gazing intently into the fire, while Jake continued his talk as he cleared the dishes from the small table and began to wash them. As he scrubbed and cleaned he talked about the Master in such a familiar strain that Jim felt as if he were some relation; that he also had some claim upon His sympathies, and would work gladly for him. The dishes were cleaned and the room swept, and then Jake joined him beside the stove.

"Ay, Jim, many a time I hae crossed these prairies thinking I was pretty smart, but I tell ye I found my

2

match. I could ride faster and better'n any of the
boys, 'n, thinks I, there's none can beat me, I'm boss
o' the ranches. Wall, I wus a ridin' to the ranch
one day, an' as I wus a crossin' the Belly River I
thought I heard a voice out o' the bush calling my
name. It wasna the same as the boys call me, but
the voice cried, 'Johnnie!' Wall, it wasna the
name that struck me so much as the voice. I says
to mysel', 'I ken that voice.' When I got across the
river I went into the bush, and agen I heard my
name called out, 'n I says, 'Hullo!' but I heard
nothin', till the third time I was a listenin', an'
then fainter so I could hardly catch it, it said,
'Johnnie!' I turned my horse's head to go to the
mountains, but, wud ye believe it, the beast wudna
go. I got a kind o' skeered, 'n says I, 'There must be
some ghosts here.' I dinna believe in such things, so
I drove the spurs into my horse, but he wudna
go : so, jest to see the end o' the thing, I let him take
his own way, an' I gie him the lines an' let him go.
He turned right to the river an' crossed back an' off
as fast as he could go. 'The spirits hae got him
sure,' says I. But as he went on, I began to think,
an', puttin' the voice an' the horse's gait together, I
says, 'I'll see the end o' this.'

My horse took me right to the Missouri River, an'

without thinkin' what I was doin', I put him in a herd an' stepped on a boat, an' off I went down the Big Muddy. I couldna tell ye all my queer journey, for I wasna mysel'. Wall, I landed at last in a wee bit of a town, an' as I wus goin' up the street, I thinks to myself, I hae seen some o' these things afore. I stopped at a door to pick up a wee thing that was cryin', an' when I was talkin' to it, an old man comes to me, an' holdin' out his hand, he says, 'I'm glad ye're come. She's been a lookin' fur ye, an' she'll be right glad to see ye, fur she canna last long.' I looked at him an' shook my head. 'Come in, John Fraser,' says he, and I looked. I didna ken what to say. That was the first time fur many long years that I'd heard my name. I had almost forgotten it mysel'. I went into the house. It was none o' yer shanties, but a fine big house: an', as I went in, the old man took me to the bed, an' he says, 'He's come! Didna I tell ye that yer dreams an' prayers would all come true?'

"'Johnnie! Johnnie!'"

Broncho Jake stopped. The tears were coursing down his cheeks, and his lips were quivering with intense emotion.

"It was my mither, Jim. I hadna ben back since I ran away when I wus a wee fellow, an' I had forgotten all about them, an' I didna ken which way to

find them, an' here I was at last!   That voice at the
river brought me to her bedside.   She took my hands
in hers an' says,

"'Johnnie, He'll be a true friend to ye.'

"'He's too old, mither, to be any use to me.   He
wouldna make a cowboy : he's too old.'

"'Oh, Johnnie,' says she, 'dinna talk in that way.   I
hae trusted in Him since I wus a wee lassie, and He'll
no leave me noo when I'm crossin' the Jordan.'

"'Mither, I'll tak ye across the Jordan if it's no
too deep.   Mony a time I hae crossed the Kootenay
an' the Saskatchewan, an' if the Jordan's no wider
an' deeper an' them I can tak ye across.   He's too
old to tak ye o'er the water.'

"'Johnnie, Johnnie! my laddie! hae ye forgotten
all I taught ye at my knee?' says my mither to me.

"Wall, Jim, she talked to me till I couldna see, fur
my eyes were fu' of tears.   The dear old body took
me by the hand as she prayed for me wi' her dying
breath, and afore she went away she says, ' Ye'll serve
him, Johnnie?' an' I put my hand in hers, and I
couldna say anything, but jest kissed her old cheek
afore she died.   'Meet me yonder, Johnnie,' she said,
and then she closed her eyes.

"I got a fine stone an' put it at her grave, an' I got
the fellow who made it to cut out on it a saddle and

a pair o' spurs, and above them the words, ' Meet Me Yonder.'

" Late one night I went to her grave an' got down beside it, an' wud ye believe it, I prayed and I says, ' Maister, Maister, I'll serve ye! I'm no happy here, an' I'll gang back to the ranch and serve ye.'

" I went again next morning to take a last look at the grave, and then I said: ' I'm off to the mountains to serve Him.'"

Jim was deeply interested. Jake had never opened his mind so freely to anyone. When he had finished there were tears in Jim's eyes.

" Jake, I had a mother, and she wus a good un. Her prayers were short, but I tell ye they were to the point. She was what some o' the folks called a Gospel liver, not a Gospel talker. When I wus a boy there wus two kinds of religion—the livers and the talkers. The talkers had bigger churches an' bigger crowds, an' the folks said they wus fine on Sunday; but ye had to look out when you wus dealin' with them on Monday. The livers were fine folks all the week, an' ye could trust them."

" Just like our bronchos," said Jake. " Christians are like bronchos, Jim. If they're well broken in when they're young they'll be steady, an' if ye break them to ride or drive it's all the same to them, if ye

train them right. Now, there are some Christians
that have never been broken in right. Sometimes
they'll balk, an' it's no their fault, they were trained
wrong. An' there are some kickers. Wall, the fellows that broke them in are to blame, not the kickin'
Christians: they were na broken in right. There are
some Christians that shy at a prayer because some
fellow didna pray like them, or they shy at some
Christian in their churches just like a horse at a piece
of paper or an engine on a railroad. Then there are
some Christians like our bucking horses, they won't
work. Ye can't put a saddle or harness on 'em, an'
they're fat, sleek an' strong. They all want to be
bosses an' feed on the best without doing any work.
Wall, they're not to blame. It's the fellows wha
breaks 'em in that causes all the trouble. Gie me a
steady Christian, a good stepper, sure-footed, well-
built for saddle or to draw, not a genteel, high-spirited
nervous thing, but one full of life, well broken in,
willin' to work and wha kens his boss. I don't like
yer dreachy Christian, allus going into his neighbor's
field or corral, an' I don't want them that won't stay
in their own band, but are allus runnin' on their
neighbors.

"I hae, like you, Jim, met some queer folks in my
day, jest like the horses I hae handled. Once I wus

boss of a ranch, an' I had some fine bands of horses, but there wus one band that beat me. I wus kept in the saddle most o' the time lookin' after them. I had a fine black horse called Scottie : he stood sixteen an' a half hands high, an' was as sober as a judge, but would ye believe me, I couldna keep him at hame. He would stray away every chance he got, an' I allus found him in a band called the Methodist band. They got the name frae the way in which they worked thegither. You never saw the like ; wheniver they were hitched up thegither they would pull for all they wus worth. They would keep step and pull well. When they came to a hill they bent down their heads, and afore ye could get yer breath they had the load on the top o' the hill. Whenever they were put out on the range they wud run and toss up their heads, an' kick an' whinny. They were all so full of mischief, an' man, they seemed to like each ither that well you couldna part them. Once in a while they would stampede, and then for several days they wouldna look into each ither's faces, they seemed sae ashamed. There wus nothing in it ; it wus purely good spirits. They wur sae full o' life they didna ken what to do. Wall, Scottie wud stray into the Methodist band, an' I wusna pleased, fur I saw that the boss o' the ranch wud like to get him, and whenever Scottie wus with the band the cowboys drove the whole band onto the finest pasture on the range. Fur a long time I couldna mak out what attractions wus there, fur I wus sure Scottie wus a sensible animal. I found out the secret from one o' the cowboys. This fellow wus a particular friend of mine, so he told me. There wus a fine mare in the band that Scottie had taken up wi', an' the two got to like each ither that much ye could hardly separate them.

"'Buy her,' says my friend, 'she's a fine animal, then ye can keep Scottie at hame.'

"Wall, it was hard work, as the Methodist boss didna like to part wi' the mare, but I paid him a big price, an' so I wus able after that to keep Scottie in his ain band."

Jim was deeply interested in Jake's style of preaching. He seemed to understand him easily and it suited him well.

"Yer mother was a good un," said Jim. "If we wus only as good as our mothers we'd be the pick o' the prairie."

The two men sat talking together over matters pertaining to their welfare, temporal and eternal, and after Jake had attended to his horse he knelt in prayer, pouring out his heart for Jim and himself. It was a simple prayer, short and pointed:

"O Lord, ye ken Jim and me. We're no strays, fur we belong to yer band, but we don't keep in the trails every day, an' we sometimes steal pretty close to the devil's range. It's no because there's good feed, but we get lazy, and afore we open our eyes to look up, we're right close on his boundary. Lord, keep us frae wanderin' in that way. It's no to our credit, fur ye're a kind Maister. O Lord, corral the cowboys an' make them yer ain. Some belong to the devil, fur I've seen his brand on them, an' some are mavrocks. They're kind, good-hearted lads, an' if ye'll be on the look-out ye can catch them, an' when they ken that ye're a good Maister, they'll stay on the range. Shelter the poor cattle on the prairie th' night. Poor things, they'll be tired an' hungry wi' the round-up. Be kind to them, an' no let any rain spoil their rest, or wolves touch their calves, an' incline the hearts o' the cowboys to be kind to them. Fur ye ken I love the cattle, an' I hope some day to meet them in heaven. I want to do what's right, but, O Lord, it would be a poor heaven to me if there wur no cattle there, an' no cowboys, fur I hae loved them all my life. Watch over Jim an' me. May we keep our spurs bright, our saddles in good shape, an' our horses well fed, an' when we're done servin' ye on the prairies, take Jim an' me to yer heavenly range. Amen."

The two men then lay down side by side. Their couch was of the rudest and most primitive description and somewhat the worse from age and wear, but its occupants were soon fast asleep.

Jake remained several days with his friend. Jim was ill and sadly needed all his friend's willing care. He intended staying until Jim was quite recovered and able to do for himself, but his plans were upset by the arrival of a messenger from Sam Burgoyne's shanty demanding his help there. Sam's babe was lying very nigh to death, and having learned that Broncho Jake was at Jim's shack, Sam sent a young Indian lad to fetch him.

Questioning the lad, Jake gathered that the child was very ill. He saddled his horse and set out at once. He had only a few miles to ride, but when he reached the shanty and looked at the child, he saw that his knowledge was not sufficient to save it. It was beyond human aid. Jake sat down, and by kind, sympathetic words and prayer did his best to comfort the parents.

The mother was a Blood Indian woman and the father a white man. She understood the English language, although she did not speak it well or frequently. Her husband understanding the Indian tongue, she talked to him in it while he conversed with her in English. In this way they understood each other perfectly, though practising little in the use of the tongue spoken by the other.

As Jake sat beside the bed of the dying child and offered his simple prayers, asking that the blessing of the Father of men might rest on the wee lamb, he thought what a pretty babe it was, and realized something of the pride the mother felt in her darling, and his heart went out in sorrow for them as they watched the ebb tide in the life of the child they loved.

As her eyes closed, Jake fell upon his knees. He could say nothing to the poor father and mother, his heart was too full; there were tears in his eyes as, taking their hands in his, he offered up the following short but touching prayer: "Lord, take the wee lamb to yer ain fold, where she'll be safe frae the wolves an' the winter's snow. Come yersel' an' comfort the hearts o' my comrades here who hae lost their lambie. Feed them wi' yer ain hand. Corral them in dangerous times. We are puir folk, but ye're our friend an' ye ken what we say. Dinna furget us an' pass us by, but brand us well an' then ye'll know yer ain. Amen."

As Jake rose from his knees he said gently, "The lambie's gone!" and then with true refinement of feeling he turned aside that the bereaved parents might give way to their grief unwatched.

The Indian mother wept bitterly when she saw that life had fled, but after the first paroxysm of grief had spent itself, she set to work to prepare her darling for its last resting-place.

Jake beckoned to the father and led the way out of the room. After a few moments' consultation they went out on the prairie together to choose a spot not far from the shanty for the grave.

Like the women of many of the Indian tribes, this poor mother had been accustomed to see her dead placed upon a platform supported by poles and raised upon the prairie some eight or ten feet from the ground; and knowing how hard it is to give up old customs, Jake was anxious to make the new mode of burial as attractive as possible to the feelings of the mother. He chose a beautiful spot, and, being a strong man, soon had a neat grave dug. He then returned to the shanty and found the woman had wrapped her babe in a fine blanket, and with it for a covering was going to have the child buried. Jake bade her wait a little while. In a few hours he had made a handsome coffin and placed the babe in it.

The little funeral procession went to the grave, and after laying the coffin in it, Jake said a few words of love and faith—words that were listened to and understood by his hearers, who could live only up to the light they had been given. They put a fence around the grave, and Jake set up a board at the head of it, on which he wrote the name and age of the child. The little one had not lived long, but she had not lived in vain. As a beautiful flower of the prairie, she had come in the spring-time and bloomed through the glad summer, filling the home with sunshine and happiness until summer came again. Then the playthings were laid aside and the stricken child lay down to rest.

Jake often visited the desolate home, and was able to lead the bereaved parents to thoughts of the higher life, from the perishable things of this earthly dwelling place to the eternal blessedness of the immortal land.

. . .

"He's a rum one, and don't ye forget it."

"Wall, he's none o' yer dandy city preachers. A fellow can catch what he says, an' ye bet he's no fool."

The speakers were in a group of cowboys and settlers, who had assembled in one of the new towns of the country, attracted by the rumor of a service to be held in the settlement. Many of them were strangers to each other, while others were strangers to the place. The assembling to attend a religious service where there were stores not only gave them an opportunity to meet and know each other, but also of doing business at the same time. Some of the men came to get their mail and to buy provisions, and when they heard of the " Gospel cowboy " and his eccentric ways, they were induced to remain.

Broncho Jake had not arrived, and while they waited remarks about him and his deeds were bandied about from one to the other. They were still speaking of him when a solitary cowboy rode quickly up to the group and dismounted. He was a tall man and a good rider. Only a few of the old-timers in the group recognized him or guessed that he was the man they had waited to hear.

Jake, still sitting his horse, spoke a few words in the peculiar phraseology of the West, and then prayed briefly. Drawing a small Bible from the canteen on his saddle, he opened it and began his sermon :

" Boys, I allus carries my guide Book, an' it tells me the ranges an' brands an' sich like. I'm goin' to read what Paul says about backslidin' and back-ridin'. Paul wus a character. He had a mind o' his ain, an' he wasna afeard to speak. Wall, he says in the first Corinthens, in the tenth chapter and verse twelve, ' Let him that thinks he stands take heed lest he fall.' An' that means, don't think because ye're ridin' ye'll no get a tumble, fur the cowboy that rides wi' his head too high will sometimes get thrown in a badger hole."

As he spoke, Jake turned upon his horse's back, his face toward the tail of the animal, and spoke to him to start. Suddenly, when touched by the spur, the horse bolted and Jake was thrown to the ground. As he struck it, he jerked the lariat, which he still held in his hand, and brought the horse to a stand. Turning to the audience, he said:

" If ye're guilty o' backridin' ye'll get left every time. Backridin' is backslidin'. Seek the Lord, an' when ye're workin' on His range never ride wi' yer back to yer horse's head. Fur let him that thinks he's ridin' take heed or he'll fall."

Mounting his horse, with a farewell wave of the hand to his hearers, Jake rode rapidly away over the prairie, leaving the listeners to his brief but pointed sermon visibly impressed.

.   .   .   .

Winter had returned with its short days and long, cold nights. The rivers were frozen, the buffalo were no longer seen, the antelope kept well to the sheltering woods and mountains; the wolves alone roamed the prairie in search of food, haunting the neighborhood of man. The snow was deep, and many storms swept over the country, making the travelling very difficult and often dangerous. The cowboys, devoted to their work and the care of the herds, remained on the ranges. These sailors of the prairies are daring fellows, and have large, true hearts. The ranchers cheered each other by frequent visits—visits which extended from a few days to two or three months.

At night they gathered around the large stove, which is always the principal article of furniture in a rancher's shanty, and entertained themselves and each other by telling tales of adventure and repeating many an experience of their life on the prairie.

Young though some of them were, they had gone through many a scene of temptation and trial, had been brought safely through many an hour of difficulty and danger. These experiences had hardened their sinews and muscles, developed the keen sense of sight and hearing, as well as the readiness of resource and rapidity of action peculiar to the cowboy. It was a life which made them true men, faithful to their work and courageous of heart.

It was on a bitterly cold night—just how cold no one cared to say ; the experience of that winter was sufficient for any tenderfoot on the prairie—that

the cowboys at Oxley ranch were gathered around a
roaring fire recounting their individual exploits. The
mail-wagon had been detained somewhere by the deep
snow: literature, always scanty, was thus scantier
than ever, and the boys had no other source of enter-
tainment.

"Five years ago I wus working on a ranch in the
Bitter Root valley, when I had a pretty close shave,"
said Tom Jones, an industrious, strong-limbed, strong-
minded young man, who was as true and daring as he
was strong. "Those wur the Indian times, and I
wus green at the business. I didn't know when to
shoot an Indian and when to let him alone. Wall,
the boss was going away fur a month, an' he put me
in charge, an' I was getting good pay, so I says to
myself, I'm going to do my level best fur him, an' let
him see that I can work better for him behind his
back than when he's here allus a watchin' us. I wus
in the saddle from mornin' to night, an' you bet I
got pretty tired; but I wus a bit afeard the Indians
would play sharp on me when the boss wus away.
The cattle wur strayin' pretty hard, an' I got it
into my head that there wus some mischief goin' on,
fur after I had got them all bunched up an' on the
range feedin' quiet an' contented, next day they wud
all be scattered, an' I had to go after them again.

3

"There wus five of us on the ranch, an' after talkin' the thing over we made up our minds that we wud get all the cattle in again an' then we'd keep a watch on them. We started out after layin' our plans, an' after a lot o' hard work we got them on the range. We wur used up, but we wur so angry at havin' to do so much that we determined to ketch the fellow that gave us the trouble. One o' the boys took the first part o' the night, an' at twelve o'clock it wus my turn to be on herd. Wall, I wus tired an' not in the best trim fur doin' any fightin', if there wus Indians about: but I wus in fur it, an' of course I couldn't back out; besides, I wus takin' the place o' the boss, an' I had to see that everythin' wus right. I had a good strong cup o' tea at the ranch an' rode out to take my partner's place. When I got up to the spot where we had agreed to watch, I saw him sittin' on horseback, never movin'. I called out low so as no one else wud hear, but he didn't answer. It was dark; I rode up near to him. My mare began to snort, and then she gave a terrible spring an' bolted. I held on fur a minute when, whiz! whiz! came two bullets after me. Had my partner turned traitor, or did he think that I was an Indian? In another minute an Indian came rushin' past me. He gave a wild warwhoop an' made a swoop at me

with his big knife, but in the darkness he missed me.
I kept a sharp lookout fur my partner, but I couldn't
find him.   I wus lookin' round with my sharpshooter
in my hand, when I saw a tall object comin' toward
me.   I grasped my revolver firm an' kept my eye on
the movin' figure—"

Tom had reached this part of his story when the
cowboys, who had been listening intently, started and
turned their heads.   There was an unusual noise outside.   Still affected by the story and their minds full
of Indians and enemies, they drew their revolvers and
made for the door.   After a momentary hesitation,
the first one to reach it threw it wide open.   It was
no enemy, although the noise made by the new-comers
was of so unusual a nature as to startle the cowboys
almost as much as if it had been the discharge of
half a dozen revolvers.   Upon an Indian travaille,
wrapped in a buffalo robe, lay a man apparently
dead or dying.   The sound of the travaille, as it
was dragged over the frozen snow, and the loud
voices and shouts of the two horsemen who accompanied it, was very different from the merry laugh
or song of the cowboy and the swift rush of his
horse's feet over the prairie to the door of a ranch.

The three men had been out hunting cattle, and
late that afternoon while passing some Indian lodges

at the edge of the wood, several ugly curs rushed
out and snapping at the heels of the horses had
made them rear and plunge. The horse which Sam
Lynch had ridden was frightened by the sudden on-
slaught of the dogs, had kicked and plunged, and,
rearing, had fallen over backwards with his rider
under him.

Sam's companions thought at first that he was
killed, and the Indians had rushed out to see the
victim of the calamity. They carried him into one
of the lodges and the medicine-men gave him some
of their remedies; but his comrades, fearing that he
might have sustained some internal injuries, thought
it would be unwise to trust to the knowledge of the
Indian doctor. As soon as he recovered consciousness, they secured the loan of a travaille and started,
hoping to find better medical aid and care for him
at one of the ranches. They travelled several weary
miles and reached the Oxley ranch, as we have seen,
after dark.

The lads lifted the injured, apparently dying man,
and carried him into the shanty. They laid him on
the best couch they possessed, thinking only of making
him as comfortable as their means and the accom-
modation at their command would permit. Although
the storm was still severe, one of them set out in

search of a doctor, riding fifty miles to reach one and procure his services.

When Sam had been obliged to seek his straying cattle his wife was ill, and his only child, a little girl five years of age, had succeeded in finding an Indian woman to take care of them during his absence; but the boys, knowing how dependent they were upon Sam, felt that every effort must be made to restore him to the wife and child who needed his care and protection. When the doctor had examined Sam's injuries he shook his head, and told the men that though he would probably recover he would be a cripple for life.

During the three or four weeks that Sam lay at the Oxley ranch he was well cared for by the rough but kindly cowboys, and when he was able to move they took him home. Sam was not able to ride, so a buckboard was called into requisition for his conveyance. He was very grateful to them for all their care, and when one of them put fifty dollars into his hand, telling him they had made it up among themselves to help him to keep hunger from his door until he was able to fight it himself, he knew not how to express his thanks. Rough, kindly lads, they proffered their gift in so unostentatious a manner that the value of it was enhanced tenfold both in the heart of the recipient and in the sight of the Giver of all good gifts.

Sam found his wife very low, but she seemed to be comfortable. When he went round the house and into the out-buildings he was struck by the neatness and evidence of care and comfort he found everywhere. There were several cords of wood piled neatly in one place, and a quantity split up and laid in the yard. The stables were clean, the small storehouse had been repaired; there was an abundance of food provided, and there were several hand-made articles of furniture in the house Sam did not remember having seen before. Someone had certainly been taking a deep and helpful interest in his affairs during his absence. Who it was he could not tell. His wife was unable to answer any questions he might ask; she seemed to be at the point of death, and he needed no experienced eye to tell him that her hours were numbered. He was still so weak from the effects of his accident that the little exertion wearied him. Sitting down in a chair by the fire, unable to do anything except to watch the dying woman, he let his thoughts dwell upon his many troubles, while he wondered from whom the strange help had come.

Presently his wife opened her eyes and beckoned him to her side.

"Sam," she said feebly, "you have been a good husband to me. When you got hurt I thought I would die, and I was so anxious about you and Minnie. My heart was hard against God and I could not weep. I could not see why we should be compelled to suffer so much, but I can see it all now, and as I lie here at night praying I can say, 'Thy will be done!' I know it is hard to think what will become of you when I am gone, Minnie so young and you so crippled, but God has been good to us. You see how things have been provided for us while you were away, an' I'm sure you will not suffer after I'm gone. Never look to yourself, but trust in the wisdom of our Father in heaven," and she sank back on the pillow exhausted with the long speech. Sam looked at her with loving, sad eyes. He said nothing, but was thinking seriously of her words, and wondering what the end would be.

The future was desolate to the poor man as he sat thinking, his face buried in his hands, no sound in the room but the labored breathing of the sick woman. The door opened and Sam raised his head. It was Broncho Jake with his arms laden with parcels. He had been away to the settlement, and was now returning with a supply of groceries for the house. Putting them down on the table he held out his hand to Sam.

"Sam, my heart is sore fur ye," he said gently. "You an' me have been friends fur many years, an' I hae come to help ye. When ye wus hurt I wus a ridin' the range just doin' the work of a Gospel cow-boy, an' one o' the lads told me about yer wife. I wus readin' the Guide Book an' I seed my brand, an' as I wus lookin' at it I could see the bulletin o' the Cowboys' Association had on it the words, 'Pure religion an' undefiled before God an' the Father is this, to visit the fatherless and widows in their afflic-tion, an' to keep himself unspotted from the world.' Now that means when anybody is sick or poor there's no use singin' an' prayin' if there's no wood in the house. It means that if ye would serve the Maister ye're to chop wood fur the sick, mind the house, make a chair, carry in water, and get them som'at to eat. Singin' an' prayin' isna religion. The Maister healed the sick an' helped the poor, an' did all His singin' an' prayin' after. If ye havena anything to eat ye canna sing very well, an' if there's no wood fur the stove an' it's a cold day, ye canna pray very hard. Afore I start on a long trip I allus feed my horse well, an' that's how God does. He fills ye wi' the good things so ye can sing an' pray."

The change in the surroundings on Sam's small ranch was thus due to Jake's kindly, practical

Christianity. He had obeyed the instructions he had found in the bulletin of the Cowboys' Association, as he called it, and came to the aid of the wife of his friend, her helpless condition being sufficient reason to him for leaving the preaching for the doing of God's Word. The journey was a long one, but Jake was strong and happy. He sang as he rode over the prairie, his heart full of gratitude to God for giving him the health and strength by which he was able to come to the aid of the helpless. He was never so happy as when chopping wood, preparing or earning food for those who were unable to work for themselves. His place for the present time was in Sam's shanty.

When work for the day or hour was done the two men sat by the stove and talked, speaking in subdued tones that they might not disturb the sick woman. She was very low, and they both felt the approach of the death-angel could not long be delayed. Sam's little daughter clung to her father's knee, her loving, questioning glances divided between his sad face and the bed where her mother lay. The Indian woman passed to and fro in her tender ministrations, proving herself a kind and capable nurse. Jake prepared all the meals, and with kind words of encouragement he persuaded Sam to eat, and by

keeping up his slowly returning strength be more
hopeful for the future. He had brought medicine
and food for the invalid, too, and when she was
awake and could understand him, he talked to her
of the better land where she should ere long find
rest and peace.

Two days passed in anxious watching before the
end came. Late in the evening while the Indian
woman sat at the bedside, she noted a change in the
sick woman. She called the family together that
they might say the last words permitted them before
her spirit departed on the long journey to its eternal
home. As they waited her lips moved, and Sam,
bending down, caught the words, " Meet me there ";
then as he lifted the child Minnie to kiss her mother,
a smile of joy passed over her face, and she closed her
eyes as the spirit passed without a sigh to its rest.

Sam wept bitterly when all was over. She had
been a good wife, and now that she was dead he felt
alone and desolate indeed.

Sunset on the Rocky Mountains is a grand sight.
Its loveliness once seen can never be forgotten. The
lofty and varied mountains rear their majestic heads
high into heavens that seem aglow with fire; clouds
lined with silver and gold guard the topmost heights.

The lines of light and shade deepen the glory of the sky, until the beholder stands entranced with the beauty of the scene. It was on such an evening, when the radiance of the heavens seemed more beautiful than ever, that the mourners laid their dead in her grave upon the prairie at the foot of the mountains.

They placed the coffin on a travaille and drew it to the spot Jake and Sam had chosen for the grave. Jake knelt upon the ground and offered up one of his simple, manly prayers—a prayer for strength to be given to the mourners and of trust in the Almighty. After they had covered the grave they planted a few flowers in the upturned soil, and placed a small upright board at the head of the grave, inscribing on it the name and age of the deceased.

On the Saturday morning following Jake bade his friend good-bye. He had to keep an engagement he had made to preach at Macleod, on Sunday. Jake often claimed the prairie as his church, though he sometimes called it his "range." His favorite pulpit was his horse, and he felt more at home on the back of this faithful friend than he would have done in a beautiful walnut pulpit such as the preachers have in the city churches.

A large congregation had assembled in one of the

billiard halls in Macleod on that Sunday morning
to hear the "Gospel cowboy" preach. The majority
of the men were drawn thither by the report of the
strange style of his preaching, but there were many
who had been helped at various times by Jake, and
their gratitude and love constrained them to meet and
hear again the man who had done so much for them.
They were Jake's "boys," and he felt he had a claim
upon them. The singing of the congregation was
hearty in spite of the fact that there were only two
or three women among them : but the old-timers and
the cowboys could sing, and at this meeting they
sang out lustily and seemed to enjoy themselves.

A simple prayer was uttered, and then after the
singing of another hymn Jake addressed his hearers.
He would not call it a sermon, just a talk ; yet if
a sermon means talking with effect upon religious
themes, Jake was an impressive preacher. He could
describe in his western phraseology religious life as
it ought to be on the prairie. He did not, however,
always confine himself to the prairie, although he
was so enamored of it, and understood it so well, that
he felt more at home, and therefore talked more frequently on the subjects the cowboys could handle,
and that he could spiritualize for their benefit.

Christ was his " Maister" or " Boss," and to be a

sinner was to be "lost on the prairie in a blizzard."
Sometimes he took a text, but he often began with a
story, and as the men listened more attentively he
spiritualized it and directed them through it to the
Gospel of Christ.   Generally he had a definite aim
in addressing the cowboys.   He did not preach merely
to explain a text; he had always a target to hit, or,
as he expressed it, "I allus try to hit the mark when
I point my talk at the boys."

The men at Macleod listened attentively to Jake's
discourse, seriously impressed when he closed with
the following earnest words:

"Boys, it's easy work to throw a steer, but ye
canna tie him down alone.   Ye maun get the boys
to help ye.   That's what the heathen parsons—mis-
sionaries, I think, they call them—are tryin' to do.
They canna throw down sin themselves, and they hae
to call upon the Christians to help them.   They canna
all run to their call, so they jist send some dollars an'
let other folks go in their place.   That's the way they
throw down sin in Africa and China.   I never wus
there, but I heard the parsons who wur there tell
the stories, an' they ought to know.   Wall, boys,
ye know Long Sam, wha got hurt in the winter.
Wall, his wife has just faded away like a snowdrift
in a Chinook wind, an' there's Sam an' the wee lass

left. Sam's a cripple, an' now an' again poverty comes in at the back door, an' Sam tries to throw him an' tie him, but the rascal sits down in every room in the house, an' then the poor fellow lies down exhausted, and he says, 'I'm beaten.' Wall, boys, I want ye to lend us a hand in tethering the beast, an' if ye'll throw yer lariat ye can capture the animal an' corral him, so that he'll no' do any harm. So here's my hat, lads : pass it round an' drop in yer dollars fur Sam an' his wee lass. Ye a' ken him, an' he's worth more than ye a' kin gie him. The Maister will pay ye back wi' interest when ye go to the bank on the day ye want to draw out yer savin's."

Jake's hat was passed around, and although no warning had been given, and therefore no opportunity to prepare themselves for it, still they carried about with them considerable sums of money, and when the hat was emptied on the billiard table and counted, there were over one hundred and twelve dollars.

Jake thanked the boys, offered a brief prayer, and retired to the house of a friend to spend the evening. Early next morning he was seen crossing the river, well laden with supplies, starting northward, and singing a hymn as he rode.

Upon the evening of the second day Jake reached his destination with the goods he had purchased as the result of his missionary sermon, and there was peace and plenty in Sam's home for a long time.

That was an effective sermon, for Sam was never allowed to want after that day. He was able to do a few chores, but not sufficient to make a living. Minnie became the cowboys' favorite and Jake's *protégé*, and she was well provided for with so many benefactors. The mavrocks were given to her whenever any were found upon the round-up, and some of the boys occasionally brought her a lamb, so that in a short time she had quite a band of cattle and a goodly-sized flock of sheep.

. . . .

One morning before sunrise, in the early autumn, a solitary traveller was seen riding hurriedly toward the mountains, apparently on some mission. He stopped to rest his horse and partake of some food, and then he continued his journey. As he rode he sang occasionally a few snatches of song. He was well laden, and seemed to be going a long distance. He entered one of the mountain passes, and when he had reached the top of a foot-hill from which he could command a wide view of the country below, he alighted, and took a survey of the plains. Having glanced around and feasted his soul upon the beauties of nature, he took off his hat, knelt

upon the ground and prayed. What a manly countenance he wore, and how striking was the attitude
of this noble man! It was Jake, the Warden of
the Plains.

At a gathering of cowboys where he had preached
the day before, he bade them good-bye, saying that
he was going west, as many settlers were now coming to the country, and they were getting parsons to
take care of them. He felt constrained to seek out
the cowboys and old-timers farther west, so he had
decided to leave his old mission-field.

Several of his friends protested, but Jake was firm.
Lest there might be a demonstration in his favor he
had left early in the morning.

The last we heard of Jake was that he was doing
pioneer work among the miners in the Kootenay
country, and helping many toward a nobler life and
deeper devotion to the truth.

Upon the eastern slope of the Rocky Mountains
there are many hearts that remember with joy the
quaint sermons of the cowboy preacher, and some
are living better lives to-day in the shanties because
they cherish the teaching of the stalwart Warden of
the Plains.

ASOKOA, THE CHIEF'S DAUGHTER.

ASOKOA was the beautiful daughter of a chief of one of the tribes of the Blackfoot Confederacy. She was admired not only for her personal attractions, but quite as much for her gentle disposition and winning ways.

The Fish Eater's band had gone south to hunt the buffalo, and were encamped on the bank of the muddy Missouri. These warriors were famous for their prowess, and though they were occasionally attacked by the Crow Indians, and had some of their horses stolen, they were not afraid of their enemies. They were well equipped with guns and cartridges, and felt that they could easily defeat any foe of equal numbers who molested them.

It was during this hunting expedition that in a beautifully painted buffalo-skin lodge an Indian babe was born. The women flocked to the old chief's lodge when the medicine-woman announced that it had a

4

new occupant, but when they were told the baby
was a girl they grieved. The sad conditions of their
own lives made them feel keenly for the child who,
if her life were spared, must bear the same burdens
and endure the same weary, monotonous existence of
toil and misery as they. The beauty of the babe as it
grew, however, pleased them so much that they forgot
the sorrow of the future in the joy of the present. She
was fairer than the other babes in the camp, and this
sent a thrill to the hearts of the women. They loved
the maidens who were fair, or hated them when they
grew jealous of their charms. The babe thrived and
grew lovelier day by day, its jet-black hair and eyes
enhancing the beauty and fairness of the face.

It was evening when the chief returned from his
hunting expedition. The mother had prepared the
choice pieces of buffalo meat for his meal, and waited
anxiously for the moment when he should ask for the
child; but he entered silently and without any greeting, as was the Indian custom. He was esteemed a
great chief and had to maintain his dignity, therefore
could not condescend to notice his wife and children
even after a long absence.

Taking his accustomed seat opposite the lodge door
the food was placed before him on the ground, and
as he lay half reclining he partook of it heartily.

but without betraying hunger or haste. After supper
the old men of the camp dropped in one by one to
learn the success of his expedition, and to talk over
matters that were interesting to them all.

The little swinging hammock made of an old
blanket thrown over two ropes that were fastened
to the lodge poles—the ends of the blanket so placed
inside that the weight of its occupant might hold it
down—contained the tiny stranger.

The babe was hidden snugly within a moss-bag.
This moss-bag was richly ornamented, and embroidered with beads and colored porcupine quills. It was
closed at the bottom, tapering to a point, and laced
up after the babe was placed in the soft moss with
which it was lined. The bag fitted closely about the
head and neck, leaving only the face exposed. When
the mother is tired carrying her child she rests the
moss-bag upright against the wall, or hangs it up
from the side of the lodge with the babe in it. When
she goes to visit friends at a distance she rides on
horseback in the same fashion as a man, and straps
the moss-bag with its occupant to the horn of the
saddle or slings it over her back. When she walks
the invariable custom is to carry the babe on her
back, well up on the shoulders. Some of these moss-
bags are very handsomely ornamented, the Indian

mothers being as proud of them as the fair daughters of the civilized race are of the tasteful, dainty clothing of their children.

This particular moss-bag was very often filled with dry, soft moss, that the child might be comfortable and happy in its dainty nest. On the night of the chief's return it had been more than usually well arranged and laid in the hammock.

The large pipe was prepared, the tobacco and *kinni-kinnick* brought out, and after the chief had finished his meal the pipe was filled, lighted and passed around from left to right. Each member of the company took a few strong whiffs, some of the old men swallowing the last one and expelling the smoke through their nostrils. The evening was passed in animated conversation, the chief leading and the others listening patiently, adding to the general interest by uttering a few words of approval. When the conversation ended the guests retired quietly, and the old chief, after taking a peep at the sleeping babe, turned on his side and sought repose; but as he lay on his hard couch a smile of satisfaction played on his features—the stern countenance of the warrior had relaxed under the influence of an awakened love for the little child.

The old man's heart had been steeled against

sympathy and love; he had lived for so many years in the midst of war and crime, and had witnessed such acts of cruelty committed against his kindred by war parties from other tribes, or marauding bands of white men, that his heart was hardened. He seldom smiled: the joyous spirit of his youth had departed, and left him old and sad.

When quite a youth he had resolved to devote his life to the service of the gods, and for a long time he enjoyed the satisfaction of knowing he was doing right. Then came a time of famine and sickness in the tribe, during which the people died in great numbers and food was very scarce. The people prayed, but no answer came to their prayers; then they plunged into all sorts of wickedness, heedless of the evil that was sure to follow.

After he was elected a chief he had been subjected to many jealousies by those who had professed to be his dearest friends. He felt that hypocrisy was rampant and friendship hollow. The gods were angry with him, and they had leagued his friends and enemies in common warfare against him. Naturally slow of speech, he grew still more reserved and taciturn. He was, however, energetic in the discharge of the duties of his office as chief, and thus maintained his influence over the people.

The quiet smile which now lingered on his features as he retired to rest after he had looked upon the face of the child, betrayed that there were depths of affection in his nature still untouched despite the many years of pain, warfare and jealousy.

Nothing eventful occurred during the night. The morning sun rose bright and glorious: an hour later the camp was all astir, busy with the duties and occupations of the day. Amid the bustle around him the chief lay still, taking needed rest after the toil of the expedition. When he awoke late, his meal of buffalo meat and tea was set before him. After he had eaten heartily, the visitors of the night before returned to talk on matters affecting the camps and to relate the various events that had occurred during his absence.

Time wore on; day after day was passed in the same dull routine. Now and then the monotony was enlivened by the report of strange Indians being in the vicinity and by the return of the young men from hunting or horse-stealing expeditions. The babe in the old chief's lodge grew and increased in beauty every day. They named her Asokoa, and the toddling prattler answered readily when they spoke her name.

Asokoa's dress was a beautiful garment of soft antelope skin, made after the fashion of a cape reaching nearly to her feet, fringed at the edges and studded with several rows of bear's teeth and claws, so sacred in the eyes of the Indians. Her moccasins were soft and pliable, beautifully embroidered with dyed porcupine quills. A pair of heavy shells hung from her ears, around her neck a string of bear's claws, upon her wrists a number of bracelets made of rings of brass, and smaller rings of the same bright metal covered her fingers between the first and second joints. Her cheeks and the parting of her hair were painted with vermilion, and the long black tresses of the child were neatly combed and hung down her back.

Twelve years passed quickly amid the merry laughter and free out-door life and sports of the camp, and the love and peace which dwelt in the lodge of the old chief. Asokoa was still the pet of the lodge and the pride of the old man's heart, but because of her sex she occupied an inferior position and had to submit to the customs of the people.

Woman had not always been degraded, for in the early years of the history of the Indians she had held equal rights with the men, those of each sex performing their own duties and being honored by the other for the possession of sterling qualities essentially their own. But the circumstances of the Indians had changed, and with the change came a gradual revolution of the old customs.

One day there came to the lodge of Asokoa's father an old man named Running Deer, who was held in great esteem by the people as a warrior. He would sit for hours smoking and recounting his many adventures, his hairbreadth escapes from war parties of the Crows, Sioux and Gros Ventres, the numerous scalp-locks he had taken and the horses he had stolen. Although he repeated his stories frequently, the same respect was shown and the same applause accorded as had greeted the first recital.

Asokoa listened with the same attention as the others, and while she admired the old man's courage and enthusiasm, thought no more of him than any child of fourteen would of a man of sixty years of age. The chief and Running Deer had several private conversations, which invariably ended in some close bargain relative to camp affairs.

Two or three weeks passed and one day a young man rode up to the lodge door and called out the chief's name. The latter rose and went out, and after carefully examining the four young horses the young man had brought, and being quite satisfied of their soundness, he bade him drive them into his band.

The chief then returned to the lodge and the meal

Asokoa had prepared for him. He was restless and evidently troubled in mind. Occasionally he would cast furtive glances about him, and seemed to be listening for the approach of someone. His wives and children noted this uneasiness, and remembered he had acted in the same manner when he had feared the approach of a large war party of Assiniboines. They feared another attack was threatened, but dare not ask any questions.

Presently the sound of horses approaching the lodge was heard, and again the chief was called upon by name. He went out, but returned immediately and told Asokoa there was a beautiful horse and saddle waiting for her at the door. It was the gift of Running Deer, and he had come to take her to his lodge, for she was now his wife and must dwell with him for the future.

Asokoa turned pale, and startled by the suddenness of the announcement, buried her face in her hands and wept. Then trembling from head to foot with grief and anger, she gathered her clothes and ornaments together and tore herself away from the home of her childhood where so many happy days had been spent. She had admired Running Deer when he visited her father's lodge, listened with interest to his adventures, but how could she love him? She was still a child, only fourteen, and she had been given in marriage without her knowledge to a man of sixty. For the consideration of four horses she had been sold into slavery, doomed to live secluded, to wait on the capricious humors of an old man, to be one of the favored in his Indian harem.

It was the custom, and so it would be useless for her to speak a word of protest. Mounting the horse she rode away quietly in the company of her husband. After a ride of about three miles they reached the camp and the lodge which was to be her home. The women came out to meet her, and a few of her friends gathered around, but in silence she unsaddled the horse, put a pair of hobbles on his fore-feet, carried the saddle into the lodge, and took the place assigned to her beside its master.

The lodge was a handsome one, capacious, and strongly built of buffalo hides. It was ornamented on the outside with pictures painted in many colors. Several scalp-locks which Running Deer had taken from the heads of the enemies he had slain in battle, hung down the side. Three other wives dwelt in the lodge, and Asokoa would be obliged to submit to the rule of the one who was the queen.

A sumptuous feast was placed before her, but she could eat little, her heart was too full. The girl felt

that she had been wronged, yet that there was no way
of escaping her fate: custom was too strong to be
altered for her.

The previous wives of Running Deer were jealous
of Asokoa and looked upon her as an intruder, but
they said nothing, showing their dislike only by the
sullen glances they cast at her as she flung herself
down on the couch of furs, and took the place
reserved for her.

For several months Asokoa's lot was not altogether
an unhappy one, presenting, as it did, a pleasant contrast to the lives of many of the other women in the
camp. This was chiefly due to her own liveliness of
disposition, which enabled her to retain her self-
respect by attending carefully to her dress and keeping herself clean and neat. The women in the camps
after marriage generally become careless and untidy,
and in some instances filthy: but Asokoa had too
much self-esteem to so forget herself, and this pride
stood her in good stead, helping her to retain her
dignity as a chief's daughter and meet successfully all
the cavils of the jealous ones in the camp. Quarrels
were frequent among the women, but as Asokoa took
no part in these family brawls, she was saved much
sorrow and daily annoyances.

Running Deer was held in high respect by the

young men of the tribe, many of whom paid long
visits to the camp to listen to the wondrous tales he
had to tell, and learn from him the ways of successful warfare. Among the visitors who always
received a cordial welcome was Saotan, the gifted
son of Eagle Rib, one of the most famous chiefs of the
tribe.

Saotan only desired to follow in his father's footsteps, and was glad to seize every opportunity to
obtain a knowledge of the military and political affairs
of his people. He was amiable and unassuming, tall
and dignified, and had already won the esteem of the
older men. As he grew older his prospects of pro-
motion brightened. He had kept himself free from
the escapades of the younger men about him, some of
whom hated him for his reticence and apparent
haughtiness of manner. He paid little attention,
however, to their sarcastic remarks, but followed unmoved the path he had marked out for himself. As he
listened to the animated narrations of Running Deer
he imbibed his spirit of enthusiasm, and felt inspired
to do and dare noble things for his race.

During the long winter months, as the camp was
moved from place to place, Saotan spent much of his
time with the old man, and Running Deer became
strongly attached to him. Asokoa was always with

her husband, and his tales assumed a new interest to her in the presence of Saotan; and though she could not in words invite the young man to the lodge, she encouraged him to come by greeting him always with a pleasant smile. His visits relieved the tedium of her life and distracted her from the annoyance caused by the constant quarrelling between the other women.

The first months of her married life had passed, and Running Deer's affection for his young bride had cooled. The degradation of her life made her heart heavy, and robbed her cheek of the bloom of health. Asokoa seldom paid a visit to her father's lodge, as it was now some distance from Running Deer's camp. Indian women are not allowed to travel alone or unaccompanied by their husbands. All unconscious that she was doing more than pleasing her husband she grew to look forward to Saotan's visits with increasing interest, and as he saw his presence was welcome he came more frequently. Life seemed to recover its brightness again, the charm of youth returned, and Asokoa felt for the first time the power of love.

Saotan was soon drawn within the same influence, and the distance between his father's lodge and Running Deer's seemed short indeed. Saotan was in love, but dare not reveal it. The woods and valleys

might be full of enchantment, his dreams be of
happiness and joy, his waking hours full of light
and life, yet they were also haunted by anxious fears
for the future. He left his food untasted, ceased to
visit the lodges of his young friends, and tried to
restrain his steps from turning toward Running
Deer's lodge, but all in vain.

Important business affecting the tribe called her
husband to attend frequent gatherings of the chiefs
in council, and Asokoa was left at the lodge. The
horses had to be looked after in his absence, and he
entrusted the duty to Saotan. Thus Asokoa and
Saotan met more frequently: from looks to words
the transition was slight, and the story of their love
was told. Cruel custom forbade their making any
confession to the old man or seeking freedom from
polygamous relationship, and they trembled for the
result of the discovery of their passion.

A more than usually long and important meeting
of the council, at which a discussion on the question
of war with the Gros Ventres had been prolonged to
a late hour, had detained Running Deer so late that
he accepted an invitation to remain the night at a
friend's lodge. Early the next morning he returned
to his home rejoicing in the consciousness of power.
His voice had been heard and his arguments had

prevailed at the council, winning him a signal victory over the chiefs who had opposed him.

As he entered the lodge an expression of evil satisfaction beamed from the faces of his older wives. At first he took no notice, then suddenly his heart was filled with foreboding. He looked and saw that the place usually occupied by Asokoa was vacant. Inquiring the reason of her absence, he learned that on the previous evening she had gone to visit a woman in one of the adjoining lodges and had not returned.

Running Deer turned and went out, quiet, dignified and sullen, determined to punish the delinquent for her unfaithfulness. Mounting his horse, which stood where he had left it a few moments before, he rode swiftly to the coulee where his band of horses were feeding, and found his wife's among them. Asokoa must be ill or something serious must have befallen her: her horse was still among the band, and she could not have left the camps. He went hurriedly from lodge to lodge making anxious inquiries, but could find no tidings of his missing wife. Then widening his circle of search, he went from camp to camp, yet found no trace of her until he reached the lodges of Eagle Rib. Two horses had been taken from the chief's band, and Saotan had not been seen since the previous day.

Burning with indignation, his former love changed to
bitter hatred, and vowing vengeance on the young
man who had supplanted him in the affections of
Asokoa, he strode to the chief and demanded his
daughter, but Eagle Rib could give him no information of the whereabouts of the fugitive couple.

Several months had passed, and Running Deer's
anger had cooled. He had given up all search for
the lost ones; he hated the names they bore, and
would not permit them to be mentioned in his presence. He had apparently forgotten them when a
messenger arrived to announce their discovery among
the Piegan tribe, one of the same confederacy as the
Bloods and Blackfeet.

Weary of exile and anxious to dwell once more
among their own people in their old home, Saotan
and Asokoa had returned, preferring to risk the
punishment which might be inflicted for their wrong-
doing. They sought refuge in the lodge of Eagle
Rib, where they hoped to be protected by the
influence of the chief. But law and custom is
stronger than the individual, and the demands of
justice are more powerful among the savage tribes
than in any other organization or race of men. The
chief might retard the operations of the Indian laws,
but he could not overcome them.

Night had fallen upon the camp and the dwellers in the lodges were retired to rest, when three men entered and seized Asokoa. A band of men waited on horseback outside. These were the Black Soldiers, the policemen of the camp, enrolled to maintain order and execute justice. They had entered the camp so quietly that no one had heard their approach.

Asokoa uttered no complaint or cry as they dragged her out, although in times of pain or trouble the Indian women are generally loud in their lamentations. Deceived by her quiet acquiescence, the men mounted her on one of the horses and allowed her to ride behind them on the way to the place of judgment. The night was dark, and as they passed a clump of bushes Asokoa slid off the horse, and, crouching down in the shadows till her guards were at some distance, fled back again to her father-in-law's lodge. The Black Soldiers rode on, unsuspecting any misfortune, and had almost reached their destination before they discovered that the Indian beauty had eluded them. They returned at once to recapture her, but as they once more entered the lodge and demanded her of the chief, she stooped down and made her escape by crawling under the leather flap of the lodge, which Eagle Rib had taken the precaution to leave unfastened. Then she sped

5

away in the darkness until she was joined by Saotan, who mounted her on his horse, and together they crossed the river, and by hard riding reached the shelter of the home of a white friend before the early dawn broke.

Negotiations were entered into between Eagle Rib and Running Deer for an amicable settlement of the matter. The angry husband had felt so embittered against the woman who had never loved him that he had himself sharpened the knife, determined to inflict the usual punishment for unfaithfulness, that of cutting off the nose. Many instances of such mutilation are in existence in the Indian camps.

The two old men talked the matter over fully, and at last a settlement was agreed upon. Running Deer accepted five horses and a gun as compensation, and Saotan and Asokoa were free to return once more and live in peace among their own people. The days which followed the return of the lovers were very happy ones. Love dwelt in the lodge that was made beautiful by Asokoa; she lived for Saotan and adorned his home with every ornament and device that love could suggest. On his part, Saotan loved her so supremely that he never brought another woman to his lodge to share his love or supplant her in his loving attentions.

A dark-eyed babe came to gladden their hearts, a beautiful boy who Asokoa said should grow up and be like his father. They rejoiced together in the possession of this treasure, and when a few months later the destroying angel came and snatched their darling from their arms they mourned together over their darkened home.

Saotan and Asokoa had dwelt in perfect happiness for three years when a war expedition was organized to go southward and retaliate upon their enemies for the depredations the tribe had suffered at their hands. Two of these young men had been killed, and the desire was to kill their enemies, that the young men's spirits might rest in the happy spirit land.

The war party had chosen Saotan as their leader, and he was obliged to bid Asokoa a reluctant farewell. The affectionate wife gazed long and sadly after his retreating form as he rode away over the plains. They were not going to wage open warfare, but secretly to return with scalps as compensation for the loss of some of their own young men, and Asokoa's heart was heavy with foreboding of evil.

At the expiration of two weeks the Indians in the camps looked for the return of Saotan and his party. Four weeks had gone and there were no tidings. Two young men were sent out to trace them and learn the cause of delay. Meanwhile the sole topic of conversation in the lodges was the long absence of Saotan. Various rumors were circulated, but the truth concerning their fate could not be learned. Small parties of Piegans, Blackfeet and Sarcees called at the camps, but none brought any tidings of the missing men.

After many days of anxious waiting, the search party returned. Long before they reached the camp the people descried them on the distant hills, riding slowly, and their horses appearing to be tired out. The people ran to meet them, the women anxious to hear what news they brought. They listened for the songs of exultation, but alas! heard only that wail of sorrow which strikes terror to the Indian woman's heart.

The chiefs gathered in one of the lodges to listen to the story of the young men. They had ridden five nights on their journey, searching carefully for any trace of Saotan and his men. Not an Indian was to be seen anywhere: the country appeared to be deserted, and they thought it would be wise to return. A short consultation was held, and as they walked their horses slowly they came to the bank of a small stream where they noticed a branch was broken from a tree overhanging the water. Searching more closely, they found marks of horses' feet, and following the tracks, they came upon a spot where it was evident a battle had been fought, for near at hand lay the skeletons of Saotan and his men. The Indians who had slain them had taken their scalp-locks, their arms and ornaments, and the buzzard, coyote and wolf had stripped the bones; but there were enough fragments of clothing scattered about to enable the young men to recognize that the remains were those of Saotan and the party who had gone out so full of hope and confidence so short a time before.

As the young men related their sorrowful tale, the chiefs' countenances betokened the direst anger, and while they muttered and plotted revenge, the women slipped away to carry the story of widowhood, pain and degradation to Asokoa. Overwhelmed with grief for her loss, the poor woman thought only that Saotan could never return to her again, and did not realize that the medicine-women were already on their way to perform the ceremonies of mourning for the dead.

These women laid their hands upon her, and in a few moments the long black hair that had been her glory fell in masses to the ground. Her neatly embroidered garments were then removed and the oldest and most worn substituted; then, laying the bereaved woman's hand on a block of wood, one of the medicine-women took a knife, and using a deer's-horn scraper as a hammer, severed one of the fingers at the first joint. Her legs were next denuded of the handsome leggings, and the flesh gashed with a knife from the knees to the feet. The blood clotted as it trickled down and was allowed to remain.

Asokoa submitted willingly to all these inflictions of pain and mutilation : it was the custom, and she felt that she was only doing as she should to prove the reality of her grief for the loss of her husband by enduring it all without a murmur. · A few of the old women sat with her in the lodge as companions in her grief; then as the sun sank in the western sky, Asokoa wandered out over the prairie, weeping bitterly and uttering the wailing cry of bereavement, "Saotan, come back to me! Saotan, come back to me!" But no voice replied, as the wailing cadences floated on the evening air.

When the darkness fell, the mourner returned, the people evading contact with her as she passed by the lodges. An hour or two of sleeplessness spent in the lodge and the early dawn found her repeating the same sad wail for the dead. The people mourned with her, but said little; young and old hung their heads as she passed them. Some of the women shed tears of sympathy and the men spoke often of the death of Saotan the brave, and murmured vengeance on the enemy who had slain him.

The days of Asokoa's mourning were long, and at first there seemed nothing left for her but death: but time, that healer of many wounds, was here in the Indian camp as elsewhere. Asokoa was too handsome and young, of too good birth and pleasant a disposition, to remain long without a suitor. Sekimi, a dignified warrior, took her to his lodge to be his wife, and for a long time was contented and happy with her alone. He could not have had a better wife. Asokoa was devoted to her home, and kept the lodge well and comfortable for husband.

Some months had passed when she noticed that Sekimi seemed to lose interest in his home, to be dull and restless. Asokoa did not despair, but sang her sweetest songs, cooked the daintiest morsels, prepared the choicest meals, and endeavored by every means within her reach to wean him from his melancholy and make him happy. Some burden rested heavily on his heart and blinded him to all the winning ways of his faithful and beautiful wife.

Sekimi rose early on one bright summer day, and after taking his morning meal hastily went out. He turned his steps to where his band of horses were feeding, and selecting three of the best, rode away. Asokoa had a quiet day, no visitor coming to the lodge. When evening closed in she heard the sound

of horsemen riding toward the camp, and as they
drew near she heard the notes of a low, sweet song
and readily distinguished her husband's voice among
the others. Sekimi was returning happy ; the burden
laid upon his spirits was removed, and Asokoa, fully
content, hastened to prepare some special dainty for
his evening meal and be ready to welcome him.

In a short time the horses stopped at the lodge door,
and the tones of a woman chatting gaily made Asokoa's
heart beat with apprehension. Sekimi entered, and
speaking haughtily, bade Asokoa set food before
them. Greater sorrow had never fallen upon Asokoa.
Her love and pride were hurt by the knowledge that
she had been superseded by another ; love drew tears
to her eyes, but pride forbade them to fall.

The days which followed the arrival of the new
wife were a dull round of drudgery and sorrow, but
Asokoa went about her work in silence. She was
left much alone, and in time grew accustomed to her
sad lot. Always patient, she bore her trials with even
greater patience and submission than ever, but the
handsome Indian woman was not so erect as formerly
and the glow of health had long fled from her cheeks.
The old women watched her sadly and tried to cheer
her : the children clung to her, and leaning against
her knees as she sat beside the river, listened to the

tales she loved to tell them. As health failed, when too weak to leave the lodge she would lie still for hours, suffering but never complaining.

The long July and August days passed, and the cool air of autumn brought some relief to the dying woman. The medicine-men beat their drums and sang their songs for her with great energy, but Asokoa begged them to cease; she wished only for quiet and peace.

The leaves were falling from the trees on the distant bluffs when the end came. The old chief, the father who had looked with such love and pride on the face of his child as it hung in the hammock, sat sorrowful at the door of the lodge waiting for the approach of the death-angel. As the sun sank behind the distant mountains, Asokoa raised her hand, and pointing to some object which seemed to hold the fixed gaze of her eyes, her lips moved. As if gathering her remaining strength for a last effort, she cried, "Saotan!" and with the name of her best-loved on her lips Asokoa's released spirit took its flight.

THE SKY PILOT.

ROADCLOTH and pemmican seldom met together in the far West during the old buffalo days. Occasionally, though, a "sky pilot" dressed in prairie garb found his way to the trading posts or the mining camps of the old-timers, where he was hospitably entertained and sometimes handsomely remunerated. There were few attractions for men of culture and refinement in such a life; only that to be found in a free and easy life on the western plains, strengthened by the desire to do good and the assurance of success which always accompanies every earnest toiler who obeys the behests of his Master.

Parson Morris was a Methodist preacher of the old school, with few tastes, yet withal a man of culture and sterling worth. He had not only seen the inside of a college, but he was a good classical scholar. Few could handle the Greek Testament better than he, or were better versed in the standards of Methodist theology. When a lad he had found peace at the

ancient "penitent bench," and the first prayer that
fell from his lips was the simple but very expressive
sentence, "Lord, make me a missionary!" This
missionary zeal had been fed by reading the life of
John Hunt of Fiji and current missionary literature.

During his college course the keen eye of one of
the church leaders recognized the fitness of the young
man for the mission field, and a messenger was
sent to request his consent to go into the work
of bringing the heathen to Christ. His heart had
been set upon going to Japan, but the voice of destiny
sent him to the western plains of Canada, where
under the shadow of the majestic mountains he
unfurled the banner of the Prince of Peace.

Parson Morris must, like all wise men, take a
partner with him to his western home, one with
whom to share his toil and his joy; for, although
there were many who sought to deter him from
engaging in such a fruitless task as striving to
lead Indians or frontiersmen to the feet of Christ, he
anticipated success, and his heart was therefore full
of joy. It would have been needless for him to have
gone forth upon his mission if he had not been
buoyant in spirit and deeply impressed with the
great work he had undertaken.

The friends of the young missionary and his wife

felt their departure keenly, and some kind-hearted souls deeply sympathized with them, and spoke to them as if they had been banished by some edict of the Almighty to dwell in lone banishment in some desert wilderness. The young parson received a handsome gift from his ministerial friends, and Nancy, the parson's bride, was made the recipient of several valuable presents from her college friends.

While attending the session of Conference the Rev. John Boswell offered his congratulations to the missionary, adding: "It does seem a pity that a man possessed of such good talents as you should become a missionary to the Indians. You would do well on the best fields of the East."

The simple answer was, "I feel that I ought to go!"

Two days before starting upon the missionary journey an interesting though scarcely encouraging missive was received offering good-will, and containing a newspaper clipping detailing the hanging of a Cree Indian for the inhuman act of murdering, cooking and eating his own family!

Some of these kind friends who sent this letter were numbered amongst the most generous contributors to the missionary cause, and prayed most earnestly for its success.

The solemn moment of parting came, and many
tears were shed, many words of regret spoken. The
parson felt depressed when thus surrounded by so
many gloomy countenances, but he naturally turned
aside in search of one or two kindred spirits, and as
he stood upon the railroad station platform there
came a vision before his eyes, one which filled them
with tears. It was that of the heathen waiting in
thousands with outstretched arms calling for help,
while not a soul appeared to hear the cry which
ascended to heaven and arrested the angels in their
mission of mercy and love. The great responsibility
of helping men toward a nobler life rested heavily
upon the heart of Parson Morris, and as he talked to
his friends, hearing and answering their questions,
his heart was far away on those distant plains.

Their journey lay through the pleasant farms and
shady woodlands in northern Ontario, then up the
lakes of the north, across stormy Lake Superior,
over the prairies of Minnesota and Dakota, until the
Missouri was reached, when a halt was made to
await the steamer. One week was spent in the city
of Bismarck, at that time a small village character-
ized by all the roughness of western civilization.

There were large ox-trains composed of three and
four heavily laden wagons, drawn by eighteen or

twenty head of oxen, on their way to the Black Hills, the land of mineral wealth and lawlessness.

On Sunday the cowboys ran their horses wildly up and down the principal streets, firing their revolvers into the air. A theatre was in full progress, and all the stores were doing a thriving business.

Parson Morris and his friends held a service in a public hall, and while the heads of the worshippers were bowed in devotion their souls were called to earth again by the sudden entrance of a man who shouted, " Is this a fire meeting ?"

Perceiving his mistake he retreated.

Up the muddy Missouri the pilgrims continued their journey, past the extensive Cactus plains, winding in and out of the sand-bars and snags which filled the river, crawling slowly through the rapids, passing vast herds of buffalo and bands of Indians, until after ten days' sailing in the famous river steamer, the *Key West*, they landed at Benton, the head of navigation. Dirt, drink and depravity were the chief features of the village in the buffalo days. Money was abundant, and so were gamblers. The main street was lined with taverns and gambling-hells, and every morning the street was almost paved with playing cards. Here were men of quality and culture mingling with the scum of society around the tables.

Brawls were common occurrences, and not infrequently were attended with the death of one or more of the participants.

At Benton an outfit was purchased, and Parson Morris with his wife Nancy embarked in a "prairie schooner" for their home across the plains. Bidding farewell to the last evidences of civilization, they began their march. Alkali lands were abundant and water was scarce; indeed, water fit to drink was seldom found, and frequently the travellers had to seek a stagnant pool, containing not more than a pailful of slimy liquid. By filtering it through a handkerchief the water was strained and freed from most of its obnoxious ingredients. At times a tiny rain pool served to yield a small supply of water. Strong coffee was made with it in order to destroy the discoloration of the water and its nauseous properties. Mosquitoes and swollen rivers served not too pleasantly to relieve the monotony of the trip. There was excitement, too, as for instance when the wagon-box was lashed with a hide and made to serve as a boat, the occupants trembling for their safety as the rudely made craft was borne wildly down the turbulent stream.

Arrived at their destination a very primitive log structure was sufficient to afford the parson and

Nancy a place of rest and shelter from the inquisitiveness of the too neighborly Indians. It was a rude building, but there was joy in it arising from the consciousness of duty done for God and man.

The field of operation, embracing an extent of territory larger than the whole of England, was extensive enough to engage all the young man's powers.

The suit of broadcloth was discarded for one of buckskin, long top boots and a sombrero (a hat with a brim of very wide dimensions). Nancy was compelled sometimes to remain at home while her husband visited the lone and distant settlements. These visits often involved an absence of some weeks from his home, and brought trying times for Nancy; many an anxious hour was passed as she lay at night thinking of the parson asleep upon the prairie at a long distance from any habitation and having no companion save his faithful horse, while the savage dogs howled around her home and the Indians sang and shouted at their heathen feasts. When Parson Morris started out on a journey, his thoughtful wife made extra hard buns, put some tea in one small sack, a supply of sugar in another, a little butter in a can, the whole neatly arranged so that it could be equally divided and fastened on the back of the saddle

" He built a fire and then hastily cooked his meal."

A small axe and an old kettle, a few books, a picket-pin and a rope completed the outfit. Dressed in his buckskin suit, the parson gave Nancy a kiss, breathed a prayer for their mutual protection, sprang into the saddle, dashed through the river and sped across the prairie at a rapid pace, for he must travel forty miles before night overtakes him. Half of his day's journey completed, he unsaddled his faithful animal, picketed her in a good spot where there was some choice buffalo grass, built a fire of such material as he could gather, and then hastily cooked his meal.

A rest of two hours was taken before his journey was continued. When night approached he sought some low lying spot where water might be obtained, and there, encouraged by a few shrubs or good feed for his mare, he encamped for the night. He picketed the mare at a short distance, so that if she became restless he could hear her, for she was apt to become fractious through the presence of Indians or wolves. His saddle was his pillow, the saddle-blanket a covering, and before lying down for the night he surveyed the prairie on every side, took care the fire he had kindled to cook his supper did not spread, and then breathing out a prayer for Nancy, he rolled himself in his saddle-blanket, laid his gun and revolver by his side, and was soon in a sound sleep.

The parson was a brave man and always found ready access to the homes of the old-timers, sharing their beds and meals. He sympathized with them in their trials, and strove to present to them the noblest type of a masculine Christianity. He was to these men a "sky pilot" and a "gospel grinder," a man whom they loved because he could ride well, swim the rivers, endure the cold, sleep on the prairie or in a miner's shack, preach an honest sermon, was not afraid to tell them of their vices, and showed himself a faithful dispenser of "soul-grub." He could preach in a tent or Indian lodge, a wagon or an old shack. He was not averse to sitting down to listen to the tales of prairie life told by the rough settlers, and at such times their conversations were bereft of any vulgarisms—not an oath ever falling from their lips or an immoral allusion, although these might have originally formed part of the tale. Willingly did he write their letters home, and carry them a hundred miles or more as he journeyed eastward, that they might be sent safely on their way. The tears sometimes came to the eyes of the gamblers as they talked together of their childhood's early years and of the old folks at home.

Two or three years of western life had passed when the parson, one Sunday evening, announced from his

primitive-looking pulpit in the little log building
which served as a school-house and church, that on
the following Sunday he would preach a temperance
sermon. A buzzing noise arose in the congregation,
indicative of the tone of feeling on the question of
whiskey and liberty.

There was abundance of liquor among the white
men, although the Indians were not allowed to receive
any, an exception rigidly enforced by the vigilant
efforts of the Mounted Police.

Sunday evening came, and the little church was
filled to overflowing. Indians and half-breeds stood
around the door and looked in at the windows, their
forms darkening the place. Within the building
were Mounted Police officers and constables, whiskey
traders, cowboys, gamblers, half-breeds and Indians,
men from different countries, educated and ignorant,
some who were graduates in arts from Oxford and
Cambridge, and others who were trained at the horse
ranches of Montana, Idaho and Mexico. There were
two white ladies present, the only females in the congregation. Assembled together with bowed heads
were men of various creeds and no creed, Protestants
and Roman Catholics, Anglicans and Dissenters, Uni-
tarians, Baptists, Presbyterians, Methodists, atheists,
representatives of almost every known sect.

The parson gave out the hymn and led the singing, every member of this strange congregation joining in the service by singing or assuming a reverent attitude, and then silently every head was bowed while prayer ascended to the throne of heaven. An able temperance sermon was preached, and was listened to with deep attention and gravity. When it was finished, and as the parson took up his hymn-book to announce the closing hymn, an aged Indian chief named Manistokos arose and addressed the congregation. As he stood up to speak, a half-breed who was employed as Government interpreter, drew near to interpret the speech of the Indian chief.

With head erect and in a clear, distinct tone of voice, Manistokos spoke and the interpreter translated : " I am glad to hear the words of the praying man. Many years ago we had fine clothes, good buffalo-skin lodges, lots of food, and we were contented and happy. The white men came and brought whiskey with them, and then our people began to die. The buffalo went away. We had no food, our lodges became old and unfit for use, our clothes dropped off our bodies, and there was nothing left us but to go to our graves. We are now poor, depending upon the Government for food, having poor clothing and sad hearts. We are now so poor that we have no whiskey, for since the Mounted Police came they have drank all the whiskey and there is none left for us."

The eyes of the Mounted Police flashed fire as the old chief sat down amid the laughter and applause of the audience.

Parson Morris arose and said in dignified tones: " My friends, we are always glad to hear what anyone has to say, but when any white men have not the courage of their convictions, but must employ an Indian for their mouthpiece, we will not listen to what they may wish to say. If there are any here who think that upon choosing the side of intemperance they have truth and justice on their side, I will give them an opportunity to air their opinions. They can have the use of this church every alternate night this week, and I will kindle the fire and light the lamps myself, as I have to be sexton and preacher; but I reserve for myself the right of replying upon the alternate evenings of this week."

There was no reply and the service closed.

Upon investigation by the Mounted Police it was found that the interpreter had been employed by some of the members of the whiskey fraternity to interpret falsely, and the aged chief had been induced to be present to give his views on the temperance question, which were all in favor of the total suppression of the traffic.

The Government authorities dismissed the interpreter, and the cause of temperance was strengthened by the brave words and manly attitude of the parson and the Indian chief.

The little village of Mackleton, in which Parson Morris and Nancy took up their residence, consisted of a few log buildings with mud floor and mud roof, and with one street of various widths and very circuitous. Sunday was the most important day of all the week. It was then that the Mounted Police started on their long journeys, no doubt being better able to reckon from that day than any other.

Sunday morning came, and the parson and Nancy paid their usual visits to the Indian lodges and homes of the half-breeds. As they went from house to house, they found it well-nigh impossible to cross the street, an ox-train having come to the village on Saturday and encamped in the middle of the thoroughfare. There stood the long trains of wagons, the yokes of oxen, and the camping outfit of the teamsters, who were at this time squatted on the ground eating their breakfast, which they had cooked by means of a fire made in the street. The men had slept in their wagons where they stood, and the oxen were grazing

on the prairie, herded by one of the men belonging to
the train.

As soon as the meal was over, the train-boss proceeded to unload his goods, and the men entered
heartily into the work, which kept them busily
engaged for two days. The work of visitation was
kept up all forenoon, save an hour for school, when
there assembled the half-breed and Indian children
belonging to the Sarcee, Blood, Piegan, and Blackfoot
tribes.

Amongst the number was an obstreperous boy of
six years, whom the parson had to seize and carry on
his back to school, and when once he had him there,
was compelled to lock the door to keep him from
retreating.

During the afternoon the bowling-alley and billiard tables were well patronized, the stores were well
filled with buyers of all kinds, the blacksmith busily
plied his trade, and a more lively day was not to be
found during the week. The day wore on, bereft of
its sacredness and peace, no songs of Zion stealing
upon the ears, and no worshippers in their best attire
wending their way to the house of God.

Four weeks had passed away and there had been
no signs of the mail. Many wistful eyes scanned the
prairie to catch, if they might, a glimpse of the

long-expected wagon with its precious contents of joy and sorrow from friends in the far distant cities of the East. The old-timers became excited and climbed on the roofs of the houses with glasses in their hands to scan the horizon, hoping they might see the rig coming.

"The mail! The mail!" shouted Kanrin and his friends as they stood upon the mud roof of the solitary hotel, and the shout was echoed from one end of the village to the other, each man as he heard the cry joining in the announcement till it had passed from mouth to mouth. The gamblers left their cards and the billiard tables were vacated as from every house and store the people rushed to gaze upon the wagon which held the mail. Every heart was agitated, and it was impossible to eat, drink, work, play or rest at such an important time.

It was the hour of holding service and Parson Morris and Nancy repaired to the little church, but not a soul was there. They waited patiently until a single straggler entered to join in the worship of God. The preacher gave his best sermon to Nancy and her companion, who pronounced it very good and appropriate to the occasion. The congregation had deserted the church, the most frequent worshippers being found upon their knees at the principal store, where, the mail having been emptied on the floor, they were aiding in the assortment of the letters, papers and books. It was a feast day to many in the village as they read again and again the news from home; but there were some sad hearts among them—those who came expecting a letter and whose expectations were not fulfilled.

Here stood a rough gambler with tears in his eyes as he held in his hand a sheet of paper written in a very trembling hand, and there upon a bale of buffalo robes sat young Hanna, deep in thought, as Indians chattered in their native tongue beside him. The letter he was reading, one from his aged mother in the old English rectory in his native Yorkshire, was evidently touching his heart, for the gay young man, cultured, kind and courtly, was nevertheless the most inveterate gambler in the town. His father was a clergyman of means who had allowed his son to emigrate with the hope of becoming wealthy and gaining a position there, which he could not hope for in England; and the young man, with the spirit of adventure, had eagerly grasped at the proposal and sought a home in the far West.

Money was abundant, and as it was much easier to gamble than to farm or raise stock, he drifted with the tide and became an expert, winning thousands

of dollars in a few days and as quickly losing all
he had. He was a fair sample of many young men
who in the early days sought wealth upon the plains
of the West.

Parson Morris became more intrepid in his work
the longer he dwelt among the rough settlers. These
men had warm, generous hearts, despite the usual
roughness of their garb, manners and speech, and no
one knew this better than the parson. He had
proved it oftentimes when their comrades were sick,
and had ever found them generous and kind. Seldom,
therefore, did he call upon them for help, not being
desirous of riding a willing horse to death, seeing that
they gave so liberally to all his schemes and it seemed
to be a pleasure to them to assist him. There were
times, however, when in religious matters he felt it
necessary to resort to the method which they called
" raising the wind." Sometimes Nancy would visit
the billiard rooms and settlers' shacks to ask their
aid. At such times she always met with politeness
and generous responses.

One Sunday morning the parson went to the little
log church to find his congregation again absent as
before ; the mail had arrived and every worshipper
had gone to find news from home. Nothing daunted,
he resolved in his mind that he was not going to be

defeated. While thinking seriously what had best be done, he suddenly recollected the startling fact that there was a church account of fifty dollars which must be paid. What better service could he render to those men, than to entertain them by allowing *them* to preach a sermon on giving. No sooner thought of than the parson started for the billiard-hall and hotel of Kamusi.

A veteran of the prairie whose civilized appellation was shrouded by his western cognomen, Kamusi was one of the parson's right-hand men. He would get drunk and swear, and he lived with an Indian woman, but nothing was thought of these things in those early days, when parsons were few and life was held to be of little value. Brave and kind, no hungry man was ever turned from his table because he had not the wherewithal to pay for his meal, and many times there could be found in one of his back rooms a sick stranger cared for and fed at the old veteran's expense.

" I'm dead broke! I'll have to shut up shop. I've been losing money every day. The people are robbing me!" he grumbled repeatedly as he hobbled along about his work, coughing severely from an old asthmatic trouble, while sitting by his doorstep were two cripples who were being supplied with food and

medicine by him, and for three months they had lived
there.

When the parson's small larder was nearly empty,
which happened occasionally, if Kamusi had the least
suspicion that such a thing existed, or if he had a
rare dish or a choice dainty, part of it would find its
way to the parson's table. Kamusi was the "Sky
Pilot's" friend.

Quietly the parson entered Kamusi's billiard-hall,
where dazzling lights were burning in profusion.
Men stood at the bar smoking and talking, and the
billiard-tables were surrounded by a gay company of
young and middle-aged men. As the parson stepped
to the head of one of the tables every eye was turned
upon him, the hum of conversation ceased, the cues
dropped to the ground and every hat was removed.

"Friends," said the parson, "I have not come here
to preach a sermon, but I am on business, and, as you
all know, I am not given to beating about the bush.
I am come here to get some money. There is no man
here can say that at any time I have ever asked him
what denomination he belonged to, but have always
treated you as men and brothers, and tried to help
you in whatever way I could and whenever you
needed it."

"That's so, parson," said Paul Vrooman, a noted
gambler, who stood with his cue in his hand.

" When your comrades have been sick I have gone long distances to visit them, at any time of the day or night, and at any season of the year."

"That's so," said another.

" I have stood beside you in sickness and trouble. I have buried your comrades on the prairie and have tried to help you to lead better lives. Now, I have a church account to pay, and I am here to ask you to assist in paying it. You have never refused to help, and I know that you will help me now."

" We will, parson," said Vrooman again.

" There is Paul Vrooman, he will take the hat and go around, and receive what you are willing to give."

Paul took his hat, and passing around the tables received a contribution from each which he handed to the parson, who thanked the men and departed.

As the parson was closing the door they shouted after him, " Come again !" The words cheered his heart and made him long for the time when they would follow his teachings more closely, and forsake the haunts of sin.

The good man spent the Sunday evening in going among the billiard saloons, and the next morning he went to the Mounted Police barracks, where he found the men sitting down to breakfast. He addressed a few words to the men, who heartily responded to the appeal, then returning home, and counting over the gains, he found that he had enough to settle his account. This he did with a very light heart. Such was one of the parson's methods of " raising the wind." He never failed in gaining the hearts of the men, as he spoke to them in a manly way, without any signs of effeminacy or peculiar sanctity unsuited to western life.

Our "Sky Pilot" still retains his buckskin suit, and when he wears it again he feels the scent of the prairie air, and longs like the war-horse for another engagement on the plains of the West, where, unhampered by the petty forms of civilized life, he can talk to men who rejoice in and illustrate in their lives a noble type of Christianity.

THE LONE PINE.

CHAPTER I.

NOTABLE camping-place for Indians, half-breeds and white travellers was the Lone Pine. It stood like a monarch raising its head over a wide, unsurveyed territory—no other tree to keep it company or break the flat monotony of the sea of grass surrounding it on every side.

Many strange stories were told of this tree. The gods had planted the seed and tended it with great care. They had protected the tiny shoots from the wintry blasts and severe frosts. They had caused the sun to shine upon it, the clouds to empty refreshing showers over it to encourage its growth ; and as its tiny leaves unfolded under the genial influence of their care, they had assembled to rejoice over it. It had stood for many years a beacon to travellers, a sentinel on the plains, a pillar towering to the sky, a guiding landmark that was discernible for miles, known and recognized by all the tribes and traders to

whom the great prairie was hunting ground and
highway.

A season of sickness fell upon the people, and the
Lone Pine, too, in pitying sympathy with the nations
who honored it, sickened and died.   The people
mourned as for a great chief, and as they bore their
dead past its decaying trunk, fear of the coming of
greater sorrow entered their hearts.

One night a wild wind swept over the plain, and
the Pine, unable to resist its force, fell to the ground.
Then the spirits of the prairie held a secret conference
at the spot, and it was decreed that a daily guard
should be set over the tree, strict injunction being
given that at the first sign of returning life the
guard should report at once.

The traveller who passed the broken stump of the
old tree upon the plain might notice it and perhaps
regret its fall, but the stately spirit keeping guard
over it was invisible to his mortal eyes.   Yet he
might have noticed that the birds flitted more freely
and sang more merrily than they had ever done before
the death of the Lone Pine.

The stately reign of the monarch was ended, and
there appeared no hope of its being reinstated on its
throne in the hearts of the people, no hope of it ever
again being a guiding landmark to the travellers on

the plains. But human foresight cannot pierce the shadows of the spirit land, and that which seems impossible is, after all, only an illusion. The man laughs at the impossibilities of his childhood, and the inhabitants of the spirit world are untrammelled by the clogs and chains that hinder and bind the denizens of the nether world.

Within the decaying trunk of the old pine the guardian spirit ere long descried a tiny shoot, and with eager haste he sped away to the courts of the spirits to proclaim his discovery. There was joy among the assembled spirits. The Lone Pine was dead, yet lived.

The hooting of the owl was heard that night more distinctly, and the wild birds sang in joyous concert until the prairie seemed alive with sounds of nature's glad rejoicing over the resurrection of the dead. It was a night long to be remembered, and was rightly given a place in the traditions of the people.

The tiny shoot grew fast, and nourished by the richness of the past, cared for with tender pride by the spirits of the air, it soon lifted its branches in spreading beauty, and reared once more a stately head above the swelling prairie. Could human speech have been given it, it could not have spoken more forcibly of the joy of life than it did to the understanding of the people by its beauty and grace.

7

What wonder, then, that the neighborhood of the
Lone Pine was a sacred spot and a notable camping
ground among the Indians, half-breeds and traders.
What wonder that the horses did not stray far from it
when turned free to feed after a long day's journey:
that the Indian listened for the vesper-song of the
spirits as they drew near the spot at nightfall, and
rested more peacefully under its hallowed guardian-
ship than at any other place upon the plains.   The
Indians fear the power of the spirits of the departed,
but they were attracted with an irresistible force to
the place where the spirits of the air kept watch and
ward over the Lone Pine.

The white traders saw or heard nothing and were
wont to say that they pitched their camp at the Lone
Pine only because it was a suitable spot—one possess-
ing all the necessary facilities for a good camping
ground.

Throughout all that region the buffalo roamed in
tens of thousands, seeking and finding good grazing
ground.   While they congregated near the Lone Pine
they were unmolested by the Indian or half-breed
hunter.   This was sacred ground, and the wild herds
fed in peace about its shade.   But the hunters watched
and waited.   When the herds moved south or westward toward the mountains, they followed eagerly,

and few who joined in the buffalo hunt from the
vicinity of the Lone Pine returned without a boun-
tiful supply of meat for the winter.

Late in the autumn, many years ago, a large buffalo skin lodge was pitched on the sacred spot. The
lodge was of superior make; the skins were well
tanned and neatly sewn together with sinews by
the deft fingers of the women. Several scalp-locks
hung against the sides, evidences of the prowess of
the chief, proofs of the number of enemies he had
slain in battle, and ghastly reminders of the ruth-
less nature of the warfare of the tribes.

One evening a solitary horseman drew near, and
after speaking to a group of children playing
near the Red River carts standing in the neighborhood of the entrance, stopped. Leaning over
the horn of his Mexican saddle, he called to the
master of the lodge. A moment, and the call was
answered, and a tall half-breed, pushing aside the
door-flap, came out. A few words of welcome said
and inquiry answered, and the stranger dismounted,
unsaddled his horse, put hobbles on his feet, and
turned him loose to graze.

Donald Mackton had not been long in the country,
but he had used his eyes and quick intelligence to
some purpose; he had learned the ways and manners

as well as the language of the natives very quickly, and was already well in touch with the ideas and many of the peculiarities of the Indians.

A tall, broad-shouldered, manly-looking Scot, the buckskin suit, wide sombrero hat and long boots of the typical cowboy showed his fine figure to perfection. He was armed with a Winchester rifle, wore a belt well filled with cartridges, and carried a revolver in one of the many pockets of his jacket. A sheath fastened to his belt also held a sharp knife. Long exposure to the sun and wind had bronzed his skin, and his muscles were hardened by the constant open-air life. His keen, blue eyes were true, and the entire self-unconsciousness of his manner inspired all who came in contact with him with confidence. He was a man whose word could be trusted, whose love had never been betrayed.

Jim Howsford, the half-breed master of the lodge, was as fine a specimen of his class and race, as honest as the best of them and a true man. His father was the son of an educated Englishman who had been in the employment of the Honorable Hudson's Bay Company, his mother a beauty among the dusky maidens of the Cree tribe. Jim had learned the language of both father and mother, and knew something of the customs of both nations and races. He

was therefore almost as much at home among the
white men as with the Indians. He, however, liked the
latter better. His mother's nature was the stronger
in him, and he spoke the Cree language more frequently and fluently than the English of the white
men. He wore his hair cut straight and hanging half
way to the shoulders, loose flannel shirt open at the
throat, beautifully ornamented leggings fastened outside his trousers from the knee downwards, and
moccasins on his feet. The belt round his waist
carried the usual knife and cartridges, without which
the dress of neither half-breed nor cowboy was com-
plete.

As the two men stood talking the children came
nearer, shy but curious to know more of the stranger.
They were seldom interrupted in their play by the
arrival of a white visitor at the camp: indeed, so much
were they kept to themselves on the prairie that they
knew more of the ways and habits of the gopher,
badger and beaver than they did of the ways of men.
They had witnessed deadly conflicts between the
Indians and half-breeds, and had crouched in fear as
the bullets whistled about the lodge or the cries of
the wounded fell upon their young ears. There was
something about this stranger, however, that attracted
them, and sheltered under the circle of carts that

surrounded the lodge, they stared wide-eyed, curious to learn the object of his visit.

Jim was too hospitable to keep his visitor long outside the lodge. They entered, and Donald was introduced to the queen of the lodge, a half-breed woman of fair complexion, pretty, and having the shy manner which belongs to women trained to believe that the master of the lodge is a superior being. She wore the ordinary dress of women of the settlements, but her way of wearing it lacked neatness and taste; the colors were bright, but without the harmony so noticeable in the work of the pure Indian women.

The life of the half-breed women is a dull, monotonous one. Constantly on the move, freighting goods and furs from one Hudson's Bay post to another, or carrying for the small traders on the prairie, they have no incentive to make the lodge attractive or their personal appearance dainty. It is not, however, a hard life; neither men nor women seem ever in a hurry to reach their destination with the goods committed to their care. They travel along leisurely and in a gay mood from morning till evening, shooting any game that comes within their reach, or taking advantage of a broken axle to call a halt and hunt in a wider circle from their resting-place. The women as they go, gather the berries growing wild on the prairie slopes or bluffs, and the children play, happy and merry as the day is long. These people are at home on the prairie, free as the foxes—Canadian gypsies, full of the joy of to-day, heedless of the morrow, not even questioning the possibility of supper, but trusting to their guns and good luck to provide them with a deer, a beaver, a goose, or a few prairie chickens; or if these fail — a thing which seldom happens—a few gophers or a skunk can be made to provide a meal.

When the day's journey is ended and the evening meal disposed of, the men sit and smoke in one of the lodges, or if the evening be fine, assemble near the carts and spend the time playing cards, gambling for almost everything they possess. Horse-racing and foot-races are also favorite amusements, and a means of gambling, too. The boys sit in a circle round a peg driven into the ground, and throwing their knives in the air vie with each other in the skill to impale it with the falling blade.

When Jim Howsford and Donald Mackton came into the lodge the woman who greeted them set about preparing the evening meal. The fire was already kindled in the centre, where it was kept in its place by a circle of stones: a small opening above, where

the lodge poles intersected, being left for the egress
of the smoke. Below this opening and over the
heads of the occupants of the lodge were stretched
pieces of shagginappi—half-tanned hides cut in strips
—upon which were hung slices of buffalo to be dried
and smoked.

Reaching to these rows of dried meat Betty Howsford took several of the slices and cooked them. She
was glad to serve the stranger generously while the
food lasted, and to trust to the larder being re-
plenished when necessary by a windfall of mercy
bringing meat, flour, tea and tobacco. The supper
consisted of slap-jacks, strong black tea and the
buffalo meat. The slap-jacks were made quickly.
Flour, salt and water were beaten rapidly together,
and poured into hot grease, and the pan held over the
fire until one side was well browned: then, with a
quick turn of the wrist the cake was flung into the
air. Turning over as it fell, the congealed mass came
down flat into the pan. After being browned on
both sides, the slap-jacks were set away on a dish
until a sufficient number were cooked for all the
members of the party. After their elders had eaten
the children were handed their portion, then the dogs
were fed and the dishes washed and put away until
they were again required.

Jim and Donald lighted their pipes and sat talking over life on the prairie and the events of their earlier days. Betty slipped away, and silence settled down upon the lodge. Soon the woman's low voice had called the lads together, and presently on the still night air their clear voices fell as the notes of the "Ave Maria" floated sweet and true, the boys' stronger tones joining with the thinner treble of the woman.

In the far north, on one of the old missions, Betty had been taught by an aged member of the Oblat Fathers, a missionary who had come many years before from the old land to teach the red men the way of peace. He lived with them, travelled with them, shared their hardships and their hunting expeditions, and when they stayed in one place for a time, taught the women and children who gathered around him to listen. In his youth he had been ambitious to gain a high position in the Church, but as he read Thomas à Kempis' "Imitation of Christ" his heart was touched, and he determined to give up his ambitious desires for self and follow Christ. He joined the Order, and was sent to the distant West, to where, to those who knew little of mission work, his culture and refinement would seem to be of little service to him. But these gifts enabled him to exert great power over the natives, and drew them to the wise man with a loving heart.

Betty had been thrown into many untoward circumstances since she had learned of him, but the sound of the old man's voice seemed ever in her ears; she never forgot the lessons she had learned from his lips and through his life. With her children gathered about her she knelt by the wheel of one of the carts, the prairie sod for a resting-place, the sky over head, and together they repeated the " Pater Noster," the " Our Father " of the Saviour of all men and of all creeds.

What a scene! One for the contemplation of angels who looked from heaven on the half-breed woman and her children as they besought God for protection, guidance and grace.

The men in the lodge had paused in their talk and smoked their pipes in silence while the petitions were ascending outside.

The prayer finished, the children returned to the lodge, and removing their outer garments, curled themselves up on the skins spread on the ground in the lodge, and were soon fast asleep.

Jim and Donald sat long narrating the various strange experiences of their lives, the half-breed exulting in his success as a hunter, and the white man rejoicing no less in the valor displayed among civilized people in times of danger, as well as in his superior knowledge of men and of the world.

"Them wur fine times," said the half-breed, his eyes glistening as he recalled the past. "We had lots of game, and we never wanted for grub. I could kill more buffalo with my .old flint-lock in a day than we get now with a Winchester rifle."

"Had you ever any trouble with the Indians in those days?" asked Donald.

"Ye bet yer life we did. Many's the time we had to fight for our lives. They'd get behind our carts before we'd know they wur there: but ye see, we knew how to fight, and though some of our folks got killed, we allus had the best of it."

"You must have had some narrow escapes."

"Yes, siree! I've had many a close shave in my younger days. I've fought with buffalo, bears and Indians, and I carry some wounds to show what a hard tussle I had many a time. There's no fun nowadays like we had in the old times. Now we never have a fight worth speaking of, and the white men are beginning to tell us that it'll be better to take the scalp-locks off our lodges; but I won mine in honest fights, and I dare any man to say that I didn't kill my enemy every time. Let me see," and

Jim took a long draw of his pipe. "I think it was the year of the big snow, that'd be twelve years ago. I wus camped on the Big Saskatchewan with Bill Whitman and Sam Livingwood. We had gone out on a search party to see how the game wus, and intended to be away about ten days. We had gone east from our camp, and had seen lots o' buffalo. I tell you, stranger, it'd have made the heart of any man glad to see them. They wur fat and sleek, and there wur thousands of 'em.

"Well, we were on our way back to our camp, and had settled down for the night on the banks of the Saskatchewan. We didn't start any fire that night fur fear o' Indians, but we just took what grub we had and eat it in quietness. As we three sat smoking I started to my feet suddenly and grabbed my gun. I don't know what made me do it, but I think it wus the old medicine-man, fur he charmed me the year before, and cured me when I was very sick. I listened, but could hear nothing, so I sat down again. I was sittin' a few minutes when again I jumped to my feet, but could see nothing. My companions looked at me and listened for the sound o' cracking branches, but they could see nothing, so we contented ourselves and smoked our pipes. Once again this happened, and I made up my mind that if it came again I wouldn't stay in that spot; but as it didn't return I lay down to rest, fur I was awful tired. I couldn't sleep, so I lay half skeered with my gun loaded and my hand on it. Bill and Sam lay beside me, and I wus in a sweat, fur Bill was a terrible snorer. It didn't matter what danger he wus in, he would snore, and it seemed as if he would try to snore loudest when there wur Indians about.

"'Now, Bill,' said I, before he went off to sleep, 'don't ye snore to-night, fur I'm afeard we're in an uncanny place.' He was mad, and said he didn't snore only when he wus at home. I told him he did, but he only got madder, so I kept quiet and asked him to be still, fur I was afeard there wur some Indians near.

"He said he would, then turned over and went to sleep, and soon was snoring as loud as ever. I am never afeard, but I tell ye, stranger, when I heard Bill snore that night I wus as weak as a woman, and I could have cleared out from the place only I couldn't leave my mates. As I lay on the ground I kept both ears and one eye open, fur I couldn't forget those three times that I jumped up and seized my gun. It wus gittin' on towards morning, the moon wus shining a little, but I could not see far. We wur in a snug spot among some trees, and I was beginning to feel safe, and thought I might take a short nap. We had a long ride before us, and we had to start at sunrise. I had dropped my head on the grass, and must have dozed off when the snapping of a rotten branch woke me ; but I didn't stir, only waited fur another sound. I had not long to wait. In a few minutes a crawling sound seemed to come along the ground slow and very quiet like. I raised my head but saw nothing. I dropped my head again, but as I did so I raised my gun with my finger on the trigger and lay quiet until the sound returned.

"Soon I saw a dark objec' lyin' on the grass like a log. It was only a few yards off, and it didn't move. I'd become sure there was danger, so I raised my gun and fired. The objec' giv a moan an' rolled over. My mates sprung to their feet at the sound of the gun, but I called to them sharp to lie down. Again we waited to see what'd follow. Nothing more happened for a while, and I was just risin' to go to the objec' when I saw two others lyin' near the first. They seemed to fall deep in the grass when I raised myself. Drawing my gun toward me I fired twice, quick. Each shot told, for the objec' gave a howl and rolled over.

"There was no more sleep after that. We lay with our hands on our guns and close 'behind the

cover of the trees until the light of the early morning helped us to see the animals on the grass, and we
soon saw there wur no others there. Bill, Sam and
me went with our guns raised toward them things
on the grass, expectin' to find a bear or buffalo, but
as we got near we saw they wur covered with Indian
blankets. We turned 'em over with our feet, and as
the blankets fell off found three naked Indians, each
graspin' a knife, but they wur dead. My bullets had
found a good place, so I took my scalpin' knife and
soon had their scalps hangin' at my belt, and now,
stranger, you can see them scalps hangin' outside my
lodge."

Jim raked the dying embers of the fire together as
he finished his story, and Donald, seeing that Betty
was already asleep, bade the genial half-breed "Good-
night" and left them. He looked first to see that
his horse was all right, then taking a couple of
buffalo-skins from one of the carts he spread them
on the ground underneath, lay down on them, and
was soon fast asleep. The air was cold, but in the
West it is quite common for travellers to sleep upon
the prairie with a very small quantity of covering;
and though the thermometer may register twenty
below zero, they seldom take cold, but rise in the
morning invigorated by the cool air and the refresh-

ing sleep which can be had only by lying on the sod
of the open prairie.

Donald was up early, but he found Betty and Jim
astir when he returned from looking after his horse,
and in a short time breakfast was ready. A hasty
repast, and then the lodge was taken down and
packed with the bedding and cooking utensils on one
of the carts. The horses were gathered in and har-
nessed one to each, and the long caravan was ready
to set out. Each Indian pony drew a load of from
five to eight hundred pounds. There were twenty
carts well laden, and each pony was fastened to the
back of the preceding cart. In the first sat Betty
and the two younger children; the two older boys
and their father rode ponies, and travelled up and
down along the line urging the ponies onward.

Before commencing their journey Donald had an
exciting experience. They were about ready to set
off when Jim called him over to look at a horse he
had to sell. The beast was a heavily-built sorrel,
and stood with head drooping and a watery eye.

" He's a fine buffalo runner," said the half-breed.
" You see that watery eye. One day I was huntin'
buffalo, and a mate of mine rode this horse, and he
was so excited he shot the horse through the eye."

" How much do you want for him ? "

"One hundred and fifty dollars. He's a fine buffalo runner. He'll take you over the ground in good shape. Get up and try him."

Donald removed the saddle from his own horse and put it on the buffalo runner. The animal stood quietly until the stranger sprang into the saddle, when, as if shot from a gun, he made a sudden bound and darted off.

Out and away over the prairie he flew at a terrific rate, rider and horse apparently bent on some errand of life and death.

Onward, past bluff and coulee, they ran, the horse snorting and galloping as if in hot chase after buffalo. His rider tried to stop him, clinging to the saddle lest he should buck him off, pulling at the bridle, but all in vain. The more he pulled the faster went the horse. There was fire in his eye: the water no longer coursed down his face. He held his head erect, and the old dreamy-looking animal was transformed into a wild, daring creature, bold and free as wolves on the prairie, and exultant in his strength and speed.

The perspiration streamed down Donald's face, and it was not until many miles had been covered that the buffalo-runner slackened his speed or appeared to think he had done his duty.

8

At last he gradually eased his pace, and no doubt in his mind's eye his rider had killed some buffalo, and a good day's work had been done into the bargain. Fortunately Donald did not turn the horse's head homeward, or he might have had a repetition of the same wild ride, from which he might not have escaped so well. Some hours afterwards Jim overtook him, and was glad to find both horse and rider safe.

"Well, you had a hard ride."

"Yes, I would not care for another like it to-day," replied Donald.

"That's always like him. Every time I've tried to sell him he's cut up a trick like that. I don't know what gets into his head. Ye see, he seems to think he's always chasing buffalo, and away he goes."

The two men sat down to wait until the train overtook them, and by the time it arrived they were quite ready for something to eat.

As they were unharnessing the horses a flock of geese alighted on the edge of the lake near, and Jim, seizing his rifle and taking aim, brought down a goose at three hundred yards. One of the boys ran down and picked up the goose and brought it to his mother. Under her skilful hands it was soon plucked, and being cut in pieces was dropped into the pot of water they had hung from the tripod of willow over a fire of buffalo chips to boil. All had been done with such rapidity that within forty minutes of the moment when the goose had been killed the men were eating it with that hearty relish only healthy appetites can give.

Every member of the party was grateful that the adventure of the morning had not terminated in an accident, as some had anticipated when the watery-eyed horse had bolted, and they were consequently in excellent spirits.

The meal ended, the men smoked their pipes together while the women washed the dishes and repacked them in the wagon. Donald saddled his horse, and bidding his hospitable friends good-bye, mounted and rode away.

CHAPTER II.

The village of Latona was situated on the banks of a beautiful river which took its course in many winding curves and sharp turns from the foot-hills of the Rocky Mountains until it emptied its waters into one of the wider streams and broad water highways of the North-West. The river was navigable during the greater part of the year, but the limited population, as well as the long monopoly of the trade by the Honorable Hudson's Bay Company of Fur Traders, and its rival, the North-West Company, had delayed enterprise in that direction.

The farms on which the French and English half-breed settlers lived had been surveyed upon the French system, with a narrow frontage on the bank of the river, and stretching back in a long strip until the required area was covered. This plan had the advantage of enabling the owners of the land to build their houses in closer proximity to each other. In a new and sparsely settled country, and to a people of the social disposition of the French, this advantage overbalanced the obvious disadvantages. The French prefer to share what they possess with their friends and neighbors in social intercourse and festivity rather than live comparatively alone until they have accumulated a sufficient patrimony to be able to entertain without depleting themselves of all they possess. The result of this social disposition at Latona was a general poverty and lack of all evidence of prosperity in the town.

There was but one street, which ran its straggling length between the scattered houses, and culminated at the one store, owned and managed by the Hudson's Bay Company. This thoroughfare was not kept particularly clean: the inhabitants had not

yet reached the stage of civilization which includes
municipal officials, or the raising of taxes to defray
the expenses of the paving of streets or making of
roads.

Children of almost every age and size, fat, naked
and dirty, played and tumbled about the muddy
roadway. No town of the like size in Her Majesty's
dominions could boast of so large a juvenile population as Latona. They were not, however, all
devoted to dirt and the muddy street: many had
careful, tidy mothers, who kept their children as neat
as their circumstances would permit.

Latona had one chapel, in which the genial priest,
Père le Sueur, ministered to his people.

It was Sunday morning, the freighting season was
over, and the people were at home in Latona. Père le
Sueur expected a large attendance at mass, and he
was not disappointed. The chapel bell rang clear and
sweet, sounding far across the country and summon-
ing the Indians who were camped in the vicinity to
assemble in the chapel, and so soon as its pleasant
tones had ceased to vibrate upon the morning air,
employees of the Hudson's Bay Company's establish-
ment marched out to attend the service and join their
voices with the half-breeds and Indians in prayer.

While the people were in the church no sound

disturbed the quiet of the village street save the occasional bark of an angry cur, excited by the arrival of a horseman, who rode down the street looking to either side as if in search of someone whom he was disappointed at not finding.

Judging by the absence of the people from their doors that they were all in the chapel, he dismounted, tied his horse to a post outside, and entered the sacred edifice.

The congregation was kneeling and following with devout attention the prayers that were being offered up by the priest, as the stranger slipped quietly into the first vacant seat and on bended knees added his voice to their united responses.

The service over, our old friend Donald Mackton was about to loose his horse and proceed on his journey when he was stayed by Jim Howsford's outstretched welcoming hand.

"Come away to my shanty," said the hospitable half-breed, "I guess there's grub and a shake-down fur ye thar."

Donald had intended putting up at the Company's post, but moved by the recollection of the night he had spent with Jim on the prairie by the Lone Pine, and the adventure of the morning ride, he decided to accept the proffered hospitality and stay at Jim's shack.

The house, which its owner was wont to call his shanty or "shack," was situated some distance from the chapel, and the road to it lay along the river bank. The walls were of hewn logs, the plan a single room without any partitions to divide the sleeping from the living apartments. It was about twenty by thirty feet in size, and contained a table and stove in the centre and beds ranged as a sort of bunk around the sides.

Betty greeted Donald with a smile, and busied herself at once in preparing dinner. The children were too shy to speak, but the smiles they exchanged with each other, as well as the furtive glances bestowed on the stranger, betrayed that they had not forgotten him.

Dinner in the house was of a better description than the one served in the lodge under the Lone Pine. There was abundance of the staple of both, the delicious buffalo meat, together with venison, potatoes and cabbage, with bread, milk and tea. The healthy climate and constant out-door exercise give the people excellent appetites, and provide them with good digestions: the plainest food is eaten with a relish such as is not often experienced in cities and towns.

Donald did full justice to Betty's cooking and

providing, and could not help praising her skill in the art of cookery. Betty smiled: she was too shy to enter into any conversation, but was pleased at being praised.

When Donald and Jim had finished their dinner, the children and a number of relatives who had assembled to share Jim's hospitality gathered around the table, a motley group, as hungry as famished bears. Needless to say, they soon devoured the remnants of the meal.

Jim and Donald were joined presently by the neighbors, who dropped in one by one to see and hear what news the stranger had brought. Jim was a genial host and a great favorite in the village. The half-breeds are nearly all of English or Scotch parentage, with a small sprinkling of French, and it is a curious fact that the Irish and German are so seldom met with, that in a large community or colony of men of the mixed races, one might count them on the fingers of one hand.

The men were all dressed alike, and presented a picturesque appearance,—fancy colored shirts, coats and vests trimmed with brass buttons, gaudy-colored sashes wound about their waists, a pair of dark pants, moccasins embroidered with beads or porcupine quills, leggings reaching from the knee downward, also ornamented with beads, and a fire-bag with fancy figures wrought upon it hung from the belt formed by the sash. A few wore rings in their ears, and all were armed with a large knife stuck in a leathern or beaded sheath. They were all peaceable men, with a vein of humor in their disposition, and prepared to take life easy. No concern for the morrow troubled them: they were happy in the enjoyment of the present.

The older men among them gathered in a group about Donald and Jim to discuss the prospects of the freighting season, the results of the recent buffalo-hunt, or the latest rumors of the battle that had been fought between the Crees and the Blackfeet Indians. From such topics of general interest it was not long before they drifted into others of a more individual or personal nature, until they all in turn had related some adventure and narrow escape, some victory they had won, or incidents of the great dances they had attended when they were young.

Meanwhile the younger members of the company had separated into various groups, and were sitting upon the floor engaged in other amusements. The one which had the greatest number of votaries was cards. From the serious expression of their faces it was not all amusement. Rings, tobacco, fire-bags and knives were deposited in a heap in their midst and it was evident that they were gambling. Donald inquired the cause of such desecration of the day, but the men looked at him in surprise and said that Sunday was over.

Donald had been trained in the Puritan ways of his ancestors, and in spite of the rough life of the prairies, still clung to the teaching of his pious parents. It was not always easy to do so, but he often managed to enter a mild protest which had the effect of lessening the evil and increasing the respect in which he was held by the old-timers.

Upon the approach of night the company departed, and Donald, stretching his saddle-blanket and bear-skin on the floor, made a very comfortable bed for himself. All the occupants of the house slept on the floor in the one-roomed house, a temporary partition being provided by a blanket hung on a rope and stretched across one portion of it. This was in consideration of the presence of the white stranger.

Donald intended to return across the prairie the following day, and knowing there were hostile Indians about, many of them being just at that time in an unsettled state, he desired to secure companions for the journey.

Jim Howsford, however, wished him to remain to

a feast that he had announced his intention of giving. Donald refused, as he wished to get away as soon as possible, but when he found that the attractions of the feast would prevent any success in inducing the Indians or half-breeds to accompany him he was obliged to remain.

Donald spent the day by the river shooting, and succeeded in bagging a goodly number of ducks, geese and prairie chickens.

In the evening the half-breed guests arrived early to the feast: they had put on their holiday attire and were evidently prepared to enjoy themselves. While the men sat or lounged about and smoked, the women cooked. When at last supper was ready, and the well cooked and tempting dishes were set before them, they were hungry enough to eat with the zest and enjoyment of famished men who had reached a region of plenty after a season of dearth and starvation.

When their appetites were satisfied, not by any means a speedy performance, the company cleared the floor, and the fiddles being called into requisition, the dance began. Seated on low stools against the wall these musicians lent all their energy to providing both time and tune to further the fun and encourage the dancers. The old people looked on while the younger ones danced, and applauded any especial performance with great appreciation and excitement. When any of the company manifested unusual skill they recounted similar feats of agility which they had witnessed in their early days. The dance continued for several hours, then the guests sat down to a repetition of the feast of good things. This gave them renewed strength for the dance, which was again indulged in with the same animation as at the beginning.

Donald remarked with surprise the familiarity manifested among the men and women, and the apparent unconcern of the old people at the excessive gaiety of the younger members of the party. The women sat on their lovers' knees when they stopped to rest from the dance, and when his host introduced one of the young girls to Donald, she immediately implanted a kiss on his cheek. It was evidently the etiquette of the half-breed code of manners, and in their eyes no more familiar than the handshake of more reticent races.

The dance showed no sign of abatement as the night reached far into the morning hours, and Donald lay down to rest. He slept soundly, and when he awoke some hours later he thought he must be dreaming, for the sound of music and dancing was

still going on. He raised his head and found it was
no dream. While many lay around and about him
on the floor sleeping, others were still dancing with
energy and excitement apparently unabated. The
festivities were thus kept up in relays of votaries for
a week without any cessation. While the exhausted
ones slept those who had snatched a few hours' sleep
returned to the dance and the feasting, and not until
the last haunch of buffalo had been eaten did the
company disperse to their own homes.

No persuasions could induce any of the men to
leave while the festivities lasted, and it was not until
they were ended and some hours' rest had been
taken that Donald secured the services of a Stoney
Indian and a half-breed named Baptiste la Roche for
the trip to Brisbane.

Donald procured a good supply of pemmican, tea,
sugar, flour and a few minor necessaries for their
journey, thinking it wiser to take this precaution
than to trust to being supplied by the way with the
guns of the party. He had no desire to run the risk
of starvation or of attracting the notice of hostile
Indians.

The party had three pack-horses beside the horses
they rode, and these were likely to delay the speed of
their journey to Brisbane to some extent.

Jim was loud in his expression of thanks to Donald for staying at his house and taking part in the feast, and many invitations to come again to the village were given him by both the host and his guests.

The whole village population turned out to see the travellers start and to wish them good luck, the curé adding his wishes for Donald's prosperity and safe keeping while crossing the prairie. The cultured priest had enjoyed some hours of conversation with Donald during his stay in the village, and parted with him with regret. There had been mutual esteem and pleasure in their short intercourse, each enjoying the rare opportunity of discussing topics belonging to the more literary, scientific and advanced civilized world.

Père le Sueur was not an exception in devotion to the cause of missionary effort. In that distant field there were many like him who had received the most cultured training in the Roman Catholic and Protestant faith the universities of Canada, Great Britain or France were able to provide. Separated by many miles from men of their own nation and class, dwelling in camps, associating with half-breeds, travelling with Indians, teaching school in the lodges, nursing the sick, praying with the dying and counselling the maturer minds of hunters and warriors, these men of talent performed their duties

cheered by the consciousness of duty done and the
assurance that their toil would receive recognition in
due time. They had no expectation of earthly
reward; time and all the vanities of the world were
to them unreal things, while the spiritual and eternal
were esteemed all that were worth striving for in this
life. Imbued with this spirit Père le Sueur was
happy in his work and surroundings. Yet though
content to dwell among the ignorance, idleness and
filth of a half-breed and Indian settlement, he was
grateful for every opportunity of hearing and talking
of the latest inventions and discoveries made in a
world from which he had been absent for eighteen
years. Donald never forgot the tale of devotion
manifested by the life of the priest of Latona.

His men had set out before him and were some
miles on the way before Donald overtook them.
Baptiste la Roche, the half-breed, was a fine, handsome fellow, a good hunter and noted marksman. He
had been loath to leave Latona so soon after the feast,
and it was only by promising a liberal reward that
Donald had been able to induce him to accompany
him. He could speak French, English, Cree and
Blackfoot, and seemed to be perfectly familiar with
the idioms of each of these languages. The Indian
was also a fair type of his race, the Stoneys, or, as

they should be called, the Assiniboines,—the name signifying the people who cook their food on hot stones. The tribe is a branch of the Sioux.

Bearspaw was true to those who employed and trusted him, and could be relied upon implicitly to serve their best interests. A man of light build and lithe, quick movements, he was brave and looked upon by his tribe as invincible. As leader of war parties he had never been defeated in battle, nor had he ever turned his back on a foe, and his warriors, animated by his ability and courage as a leader, had followed him to victory in all their skirmishes on the plains.

The three men were well armed: each carried a Winchester rifle, a large knife, a revolver and a belt with cartridges. They were thus prepared for any emergency.

It was late in the afternoon when the party started. They wished to reach a spot in a wood where there was a good camping ground, about twenty miles distant, before night. To accomplish this they had to ride fast, but were not able to make great speed owing to the necessity of attending to the pack-horses. Intent upon reaching their destination and the shelter of the wood before the sun went down, the party rode in silence. It was dusk when they at last drew rein, and after casting a sharp glance around to see that the ground was clear and no trace of enemies visible, they dismounted, loosened the packs, hobbled the horses and made a fire.

Donald lay on his saddle-blanket while Baptiste and Bearspaw bustled about preparing the supper. There was no delay in arranging the table, and seated upon the grass the tired men ate heartily of the pemmican, slap-jacks and strong black tea.

"Good evening, gentlemen!" said a bronzed-faced man who alighted from his horse as he spoke. He had approached so quietly that the greeting startled Donald, and he laid his hand on his revolver. The Indian's face betrayed no knowledge or surprise, although with the keen hearing of the native he must have known of the stranger's proximity.

"Good evening," replied Donald. "Will you sit down and have some supper with us? We have enough and will be glad to have your company."

"Thank ye, friends. Don't mind if I do. I'm hungry and I never refuse a kindness from a stranger."

"Which way are you travelling?" asked Donald, presently, when the new-comer had shown by the way he devoured the food set before him that he had fasted some time. "You seem to be tired."

9

"Well, yes, I was gone a good bit, an' I don't exactly know where I'll turn up before I'm done. Ye see, I have not had good luck with my trapping."

"Which way have you been that you have been so unfortunate? Surely the game is not scarce at this time of the year."

"Wall, no, I guess there's lots o' furs, but the Indians haven't been very civil this year, an' when I get ahead some o' the rascals steal my cache, an' then I have to begin all over again. I've been along the foot o' the mountains an' followed an old Stoney trail for a while, but ye see I'm gettin' old an' I guess some o' these days I'll have to pass in my checks, and then it'll be all over with Jim Carrafell."

The old trapper's appearance did not belie his words, and Donald had not much difficulty in persuading him to join his party.

They sat for some time around the fire, smoking and talking, Donald and Jim Carrafell exchanging experiences, Baptiste and Bearspaw talking in the monologues peculiar to the Indian. When the night fell thick about the camp the men rolled themselves in their blankets, turned their feet to the fire, and with their saddles for pillows were soon asleep. They knew that during the early part of the night no Indian would venture to attack them, yet they slept

with hands on their revolvers and guns within
reach, so that if molested they were ready to meet
the foe.

The sleepers, however, were not disturbed, and at
the first break of dawn the Stoney was up and looking to see that the horses were safe. To cook and
eat their breakfast, gather the stuff together and set
out occupied little time. Nothing eventful occurred
during the day, they met no Indians, saw but few
buffalo. An odd timber wolf cast sinister glances
at them as they rode past, or occasional coyotes slunk
away with drooping tail at their approach, but
nothing of more importance broke the monotony of
the day's ride. The evening was but a repetition of
the night before.

When they reached the halting place and camped
one evening about sixty miles from their destination,
Donald learned with consternation that the provisions
were exhausted. He had brought what he considered
abundance for the trip, even when allowance was
made for the addition to their number by the arrival
of Jim Carrafell, and he was surprised that the supply
should so soon be gone. It was a new experience to
Donald, though not an uncommon one in the lives of
many travellers with such parties. The half-breed
had feasted, eating enough for three men, as if he

believed that he should lay in a stock of food that would sustain him for a week.

The Indian, with the instinct of his race, started ahead of the party the next morning to levy supplies from the prairies with his gun, and was successful in shooting enough duck, geese and rabbits to keep them from starving.

It was dark when they rode into the village of Brisbane, but the half-breeds and Indians who formed the principal part of the population were abroad to welcome them.

Donald paid his men and dismissed them, having decided to remain over a few days in the town.

The half-breed went to the house of one of his relatives, where he was received with open arms. There he stayed for a week, enjoying his friend's hospitality, and without giving a thought to his home. Happy and careless, a true son of the soil, he was heedless of anything or anyone while he had enough to eat and drink, and was blessed with a fiddle and a friend.

Bearspaw was of a more dignified nature and appearance. He rode slowly through the village to the lodge where one of his tribe lived, and entered quietly, assured of a welcome by the native courtesy and hospitality that ever are characteristic of the

Indian races. He talked soberly, without any such demonstrative excitement as was noticeable in the demeanor of the half-breed; made inquiry after the welfare of the people and of the changes which had taken place among the families since he left them. When they told him of death in the camp he said nothing, and as they related the successes his people had met with in the hunting expeditions, he was silent. Bearspaw was sympathetic in both their sorrow and joy, but the training of camps had made him, like all the other members of his tribe and race, the master of his emotions.

Then they told him that the messenger of death had come to his own lodge three nights before and stricken down his eldest son, a young lad and the pride of his father's heart; but Bearspaw still sat motionless, uttering no word. It would seem as if they had been speaking of another. Courage died out of their hearts; they had spoken, they now sat silent.

Presently, with no sign of haste, the bereaved father rose from his place in the lodge, and without a word departed. His horse was still fastened to the pole at the entrance of the lodge, but Bearspaw seemed as if he saw him not. His heart bore too heavy a burden to think of aught but his sorrow.

Looking neither to the right nor left he strode onward until he reached a dense wood outside the precincts of the village. He thought not of possible danger; his hand was not laid on his knife as it would have been at ordinary times. Why should he go thence? Why leave his friends? Upon what mission is he bent? Wearied with his long journey does he seek rest?

Alas! no. His heart is very heavy with grief, and he must leave the haunts of men to seek relief for his wounded spirit. Converse with the gods alone can bring peace. Hidden from the eye of men he throws himself upon the ground in an agony of spirit. Hero of a hundred battles, his lodge decked with scalp-locks, the story of his valor written in pictures on the walls—valor that had never been exceeded by any that had been told before—the man who had never been defeated lay prone upon the ground, vanquished by this blow. He shed no tears, uttered no cry, but groaned in the bitterness of his grief. Then on the midnight air the plaintive notes of the wail for the departed fell soft and sad, the coranach of his race, the father wailing for his dead son, calling on his name, repeating it again and again in the curious pathetic monotone peculiar to the Indian.

When the day dawned and the night of grief was passed, Bearspaw returned in sadness to his lodge, and the women with dishevelled hair, bare feet and torn and tattered garments, bewailed the dead until the season of mourning was expired.

Life is sad in every clime; to every camp or home death comes. In the midst of peace, prosperity and joy sorrow falls, our loved ones are taken from us, and the world to us seems empty, valueless and of little worth.

Bearspaw never mentioned his son's name; his grief was silent, but his hair grew whiter and deeper furrows marked his brow, telling better than any lamentations how great had been his loss.

CHAPTER III.

Donald Mackton had spent some days in Brisbane, and was preparing to leave and set out again on his travels when he met Peter Daniels. A new acquaintance in the far West was an event of some importance, and worth something in those days. Friends were few and far between, and the chance acquaintance of to-day might be the helpful friend of the morrow.

Peter Daniels was a tall man, of an aristocratic appearance indicative of better days. He was dressed

in the usual suit of buckskin, but his jacket was more
elaborately ornamented with colored porcupine quills
than was common; his pants were made of moose-
skin and the leggings worn over them from the knee
downward were very handsomely embroidered with
beads : his moccasins were also richly worked by the
deft hands of an Indian woman. The wide sombrero
hat, such as is worn by the Mexican or Montana cowboy, completed his costume. He spoke the pure
English of an educated man, yet his face betrayed
unmistakable signs of a predilection for strong drink
in the past, if not at the present time.

Peter was a rare character. He posed as a literary
man among his companions, and expressed his intention of one day writing a history of the country, one
that would include an autobiography.

Donald, as we have said, was something of a
scholar, and the pleasure of meeting an educated man
out in the wilds was sufficient attraction to induce
him to prolong his stay in Brisbane. After a short
chat in the store, Donald was easily persuaded to pay
him a visit in his own house. He found the place an
old log building, sadly in need of repair; but this did
not seem to trouble its occupant at all. Donald went
in and spent several hours in pleasant conversation
with his host.

" You have been several years in the country, Mr. Daniels, I understand ? " said Donald, presently.

" Well, yes : I have spent about twelve years in this particular district."

" You evidently have been enamored of the people, the climate or the manner of life, that you have remained so long ? "

" Well, sir, I can hardly tell you why I have stayed, or what has been the particular attraction. I am hard to please, yet there is something in this country which induces a man to forego many of the benefits of civilization for the free and easy life possible on these western prairies."

" You were not brought up to this kind of life, I can see very well," replied Donald.

" No, I am an Englishman. I was educated at Eton and Oxford. After I left college, I took a fancy to see the world."

" You have come a long way to see it."

" Yes. And yet I have been well repaid. I have spent five or six thousand pounds since I came here, but that is nothing when you think of all the experience I have gained. If I had lived in England I should have spent much more and not have known half the things I do now. We have all to pay for our knowledge, and of course I am no exception to

the rule. My rich friends at home would be shocked
to see me in this shack or dressed in this fashion, but
I am happy, and that is the chief thing in life. It
matters little where you are or what you are doing
if you are happy. I hope some day to relate my
experiences and publish them, and that will be full
compensation for all the hardships of this kind of
life."

" I hope so," replied Donald, slowly.

" You appear to doubt it, my friend, but I have
learned much, and as it has cost me a great deal, I
think, and not without sufficient reason, that I ought
to be able to recount my experiences in an entertain-
ing manner. If I succeed, they are sure to bring me
some compensation for the trouble."

"I do not doubt that," said Donald: "what I thought
was that the labor will be too great and the hardships
too severe for the reward to be adequate. The isola-
tion, the privations, the absence of all the luxuries of
life, the loss of friends and the monotony of prairie
life—is not this too much to give for all the wealth
and fame the world is able to bestow in one short
life ?"

" That is true to you, perhaps, but we are not all
made alike, and nothing could please me more than
to spend my life for the benefit of others, in relating

to my fellowmen the adventures of the last few years."

To write a book was evidently Mr. Daniels' highest ambition, as it has been the worthy desire of many nobler men.

"Your life has been spent chiefly among the Indians, I suppose," said Donald.

"Indians and half-breeds," replied Daniels.

"Which of the two types of men do you find the better?" asked Donald. "Are not the former finer men than the latter?"

"Just the opposite. I have spent most of my time while in the country among the half-breeds, and have gleaned so much of their history and entered so fully into their spirit that I look upon the race as one of the noblest on the face of the earth."

"Your experience differs from mine, then."

"Perhaps so, but you will pardon me if I say that possibly mine has been larger and more varied than yours, and that being the case, I am better able to speak authoritatively on the question. I do not often mention the facts of my own life in this relation, but it is sometimes necessary in order to throw light upon the matter, and I will tell you as briefly as possible the reasons for my belief in the nobility of character in the race."

"Thank you : it will be a pleasure to me to listen to what you say," said Donald, smiling.

"About fourteen years ago," began Daniels, "my father called me into his study and told me he had decided to send me out to America. He would give me a few thousand pounds to enable me to start life there well and make an independent living. I was very willing to fall in with his views, as nothing pleased me better than the thought of hunting in the far West. A few days later he placed a cheque for two thousand pounds in my hand and bade me make all necessary arrangements for my journey. There was nothing much to be seen in Montreal, so I cashed my cheque when I arrived there and pushed on to the West, which I reached in the course of some weeks in the company of several adventurers like myself. The first years were spent in the village of Latona, where I made the acquaintance of the half-breeds, and learned to respect them. I found many honest and plucky men among them. There was Jack Sutherland, a Scotch half-breed, true as steel; no prouder man than he ever stood in a mansion. Let me tell you of him ; his story will serve as well as another to illustrate what I want to prove."

"Go on," said Donald, "I'm all ears."

"Jack was one of the employees of the Hudson's

Bay Company, who had been sent from one of the northern posts to the Company's post at Latona. He was a quiet fellow, reserved and proud, conscious of his strength and superior skill with a rifle, but no boaster. He was as much at home in a canoe on the lake or river as on a horse on the prairie. He dined at the long table in the Fort, but lived in a small house by himself that was situated just within the walls of the Fort. There he had a small but well-chosen stock of books that had belonged to his father, an officer of the Company. These books were of the right sort, and what was better, were often read.

"Jack was a very agreeable companion, full of information, and when among his particular friends was fond of a joke. He had all the canny disposition of the Scotch race, with the instincts of the Indian. He was daring and hardy, yet seldom did anything of an extraordinary nature, which may have arisen from his intense hatred of display. I knew the man well and learned to love him.

"Late one afternoon we were apprised by some of the Cree Indians that there were Blackfoot Indians in the vicinity, and it would be well for us to be on our guard. We took all necessary precautions, but no Indian appeared.

"Three or four days went by and we felt sure the Cree who brought the tidings of the proximity of the Blackfeet must have been mistaken. We did not hear of any misdeeds, so we settled down again to our old ways of living.

"The villagers were retiring to rest when a man rode down the street, and called to a few stragglers who were still about that one of the children of the Factor at the Fort was missing.

"The children had been playing together inside the walls of the Fort, and unconscious of any danger had gone outside to pluck some of the flowers growing there in rich profusion. One of them, a girl of about five years of age, lingered behind the others, and when they turned to call her she had disappeared. They searched for her, calling her repeatedly, but all their efforts were fruitless. Then they returned to inform their parents. All the employees were at once astir and searching in every direction, but without success.

"The mother was distracted and the father wild with grief and apprehension.

"The news spread quickly and the villagers joined in the search. They rode along the river bank and scoured the prairie in the darkness. but could find no trace of the missing child. For several days they continued to search the country hoping to find her, but without success.

"Amongst those who had travelled far and near in prosecuting the search there was one who had not been numbered. About a month before this sad occurrence the Factor had used some strong language in talking to Jack Sutherland, and it was well known that the half-breed had been indignant and had felt the reprimand keenly.

"Jack had not joined the party of searchers, and no one had seen him since the night on which little Annie MacKenzie had disappeared. Inquiries elicited the fact that he had been seen repairing his saddle upon the morning of the day in question, but no one remembered having seen him later. Had he taken revenge upon the chief of the Fort, done away with the child and then decamped?

"Everyone knew the Scotch half-breed as an honest, kind-hearted man, and it was hard to believe that he could be guilty of such a crime: still the fact remained, he could not be found. His room was unswept, the door unlocked, articles of clothing left lying about, all evidence of a hurried departure. This seemed corroborative of the suspicion that he had either stolen the child or put it to death.

"Factor MacKenzie offered a reward of ten of his

best horses to anyone giving a clue by which the half-breed might be traced and the truth discovered.

"Jack had too many friends at the Fort and in Latona for anyone to undertake this mission. Men and women were all anxious and willing to search for the child, but not one among them could be induced to start in pursuit of Jack Sutherland. Finding there was no response to his offer of reward the Factor determined to set out on the search himself. Two of the most trusted of the officials were to accompany him, well armed, lest they should meet with opposition in securing the fugitive. Their outfit was got ready and arrangements made for a lengthened absence from the Fort.

"The Factor and his men were sitting late discussing their plans for the following day, when a knock at the door interrupted the conversation, and a stranger was introduced.

"Pierre le Jeune had heard of the Factor's loss, and had come a long distance that he might offer his services to search for the child. He professed to know the country well, and had not the least doubt that he would be successful in finding Jack Sutherland and bringing back his scalp to claim the reward. His eyes sparkled with an evil light as he uttered the name of the absent half-breed.

"Pierre was a daring fellow, a native of the plains, a French half-breed with some Spanish blood in his veins. He lived in one of the native settlements, and as soon as he heard of the calamity at the Fort had at once started for Latona.

"The Factor saw by the determined manner of the man that he was in earnest, and learning that he and Jack were old-time enemies, he felt that there was better chance of successful pursuit being made by him than by himself and his officers. They were not prepared by familiarity with the ways and tactics of the Indians, as this French half-breed was, to cope with the difficulties of encounter with hostile bands, and though very anxious to prosecute the search for the lost child they felt that it would be unwise to run into danger unnecessarily.

"Long and anxiously they talked over their schemes and plans, the trails to be followed, the hope of gaining the object and the compensation to be given Pierre le Jeunne for his help. At last the terms were agreed upon, Pierre was given a good supply of food and tobacco, and it was agreed that the Factor should wait several days until sufficient time had been given the half-breed to let them know in some manner whether he had been successful in his undertaking.

10

"Bidding them good morning, for the talk had lasted through the night, Pierre set out, and turned his horse's head toward the south. There was a determined, evil expression on the man's face as he rode along, while a faint smile of satisfaction long delayed lingered about his eyes and mouth. He was in quest of his enemy, and now supported by the strong arm of the law he was at last to have his revenge.

"Keeping a sharp lookout for straggling parties of Indians he sped on, covering many miles but meeting with no adventure during the first day.

"On the second day, after fording a river he crossed the plains until he came to a stone of a peculiar kind that was lying on the ground. Dismounting beside it he took some tobacco from his saddle-bag and threw it down near the stone. This was one of the massive meteorites which the Indians are in the habit of visiting and offering sacrifices to. The half-breed having made his offering stood awhile muttering his petitions, asking for protection on his journey and success in his mission.

"After waiting a few minutes and receiving no response from the oracle, he remounted and continued his journey. Upon the fourth day he entered the country of the Blackfoot tribe, and turned aside to visit the Lone Pine. There were many offerings laid at its foot and strewn about on the ground. Pierre threw down his gifts of tobacco and waited for a response to his prayer. Presently a low murmur fell upon his ear, like the sound of distant thunder. He looked upward to the sky, but it was clear. He scanned the horizon and the low bushes growing near, but could discern nothing, neither human beings nor animals. In an anguish of superstition he threw himself upon the ground, hopeless of success, for there seemed to be opposition to him and his mission from some unknown quarter.

"As he lay motionless the sounds increased. He pressed his ear close to the ground and listened. Fear took possession of the half-breed warrior's heart. He had oftentimes gone forth to battle without fear and had returned victorious; but now he was afraid, and not without reason.

"The sound he heard was the dull thud of horses' hoofs upon the prairie. He was alone in an enemy's country, and unable to cope with them should they prove to be numerous.

"Grasping the bridle he led his horse into the thickest part of the bush, and there, hidden from view, he lay and watched the advance of the horsemen. In a few moments a solitary rider dashed past, followed at some little distance by several Indians, who were yelling wildly and shooting at random.

Pierre recognized some of his friends among the latter, and emerging from his hiding-place shouted to them, calling them by name. They turned a moment, sufficient to learn who he was, and then continued their pursuit of the solitary horseman.

"As he dashed past the Lone Pine this rider flung his offering down, and as if inspired by fresh courage and hope, grasped more firmly a bundle which lay across his saddle before him. Maintaining an even, steady gait, yet one of great speed, he succeeded in keeping in advance of his pursuers.

"As darkness fell the Indians slackened their pace, and at last ceased to follow, and the sound of their horses' feet being no longer heard, the man left the trail and sought a safe hiding-place for the night. Carefully depositing his burden he sat down to watch; he dare not sleep, although he was obliged to rest.

"Before the sun rose in the morning he was again on his journey northward. He saw no sign of his pursuers, but he knew he was not safe, so pressed onward with all the haste his horse could accomplish. Through rivers and creeks he rode heedless of danger. He was nearing his journey's end faint with hunger, hard riding and loss of sleep. His horse, too, was jaded, yet conscious of danger, and hopeful at last of rest, pressed on without any urging from his master.

"He grasped more firmly a bundle which lay across his saddle."

"But a few miles and home is gained. Yonder, looming up on the prairie, are the Fort and houses of the village of Latona.

"Whiz! whiz! Two bullets in rapid succession pass the rider, who, at the sound of their coming, has bent low, leaning forward to protect the bundle on his knee.

"The Indians have followed, and are on his track. Madly they ride, fearful of losing their prize. The blood is trickling down the horse's side and his strength is well-nigh spent.

"From the Fort their approach has been seen and eager eyes are watching the chase. The pursuers are gaining, the pursued is wounded, and evidently in sore straits.

"But he wins, and as he dashes into the Fort the watchers see the bundle on his knee and shout:

"'Pierre le Jeunne! Pierre le Jeunne! He has found the child! He has found the child!'

"'Pierre!' cried the Factor, as he took his lost and now restored darling from the man's outstretched arms.

"But the faltering words that met him were not spoken by the lips of the French half-breed. It was Jack Sutherland who reeled and would have fallen from his saddle had not ready hands caught him. They carried him into the Factor's room at the Fort, and every care was bestowed upon him, but he was wounded to the death. His lips move. What is he saying? They bend to listen.

"'I have saved her! She is safe! Thank God!'

"The Factor's eyes were dim. The man he had doubted, who he believed would revenge so cruelly the slight given him, had saved his child from a fate that was worse than death. And now he was dying, his life given for the life of the child. He had preserved the peace and happiness of the home of the man who had insulted him and believed evil of him.

"Jack lingered a day or two before the end came. Meanwhile Pierre le Jeune had returned. It was toward evening when, opening his eyes and seeing his old enemy standing sullen by the door, the stricken man held out his hand with a smile.

"'She is safe!' he said faintly, and died. The great soul of the half-breed, the child of the plains, had gone to its reward."

Donald left Brisbane a few days later. He never met Peter Daniels again, but in his eastern home, years after, when, surrounded by boys and girls, he told them tales of the West, the one most in favor among them was the story of the Lone Pine and the rescue of little Annie MacKenzie, the Factor's child, by brave Jack Sutherland.

THE WRITING STONE.

UNDER the shadow of the Rocky Mountains the wandering tribes of Bloods and Blackfeet roamed free and happy in the days of yore. The prairie gods looked down and smiled upon the dwellers in the painted lodges, and the smiles brought peace and plenty to their dusky wards. Over the prairie lay the huge stones, remnants of the mighty rock which in the distant past had chased the Old Man of the Mountains, determined to punish him for his cruel ways. The strangely-shaped trees that fringed the river, the lonely mounds that stood as sentinels on the prairie, and these large rocks were now the stopping-places of the prairie gods. To these sacred relics the pious natives oftentimes repaired, and with earnest supplications made sacrifices to their spirit friends.

Mastwena, an aged warrior, on bended knee besought help for his kindred in a time of sorrow. As he laid his gifts upon the ground and prepared to depart, there came a voice that spoke of woe in the land of the south. Silently he arose and went toward the lodges, with downcast head and troubled breast.

It was dark when he entered his lodge, and his friends saw not the sorrow that clouded his face. The moments were few which he spent in slumber. Long before the sun had risen Mastwena left his couch and sought again the sacred spot. As his lips parted once more in earnest prayer, the voice again was heard telling of desolation and woe. With a heavy heart he left the place of sacrifice and wandered out upon the prairie, dreaming of the coming sorrow that should visit the people of the plains. There came no messenger to relieve him of his grief. The day wore on, and evening found him again among his people. Four days he repeated his visit to the Stone of Sacrifice, only to hear the spirit prophet repeat the revelation so full of mystery and darkness to his soul.

The lodge fires were burning brightly upon the evening of the fourth day, as with song and dance the hearts of both young and old were filled with joy. The quick beating of the medicine drums told that the young men were amusing themselves at some of their native games, and the gambler's laugh was occasionally heard as he gathered in the prizes he had won. In one of the lodges a band of men and women were celebrating a tea dance. Half intoxicated with the large quantities of tea which they drank, they were singing and shouting with savage glee. The old men were relating their war-like deeds, and the young men were passing jokes upon each other. The whole camp indeed was full of life, for they had abundance of food and clothing, and the prairie gods had smiled upon them, bringing health and peace to young and old.

In the midst of this jollity a young man, haggard and weary, came running slowly into the camp. As he made toward the lodge where the aged Mastwena dwelt, he fell to the ground from sheer exhaustion.

Mastwena was standing near, confidently waiting for the approach of some messenger who should un-ravel the mystery of the Stone of Sacrifice, and as the young man fell he knelt beside him, raised him gently in his strong arms, and carried him into his lodge.

He bade his wife and daughter tend him, and as they nursed the young man back to life again, and beheld the strength and color of youth returning, they rejoiced exceedingly. Mastwena said little but gazed often upon the countenance of the young man, and his eye sparkled as some new thought flashed upon his mind. Anxiously he watched and waited to put questions to the invalid youth, but betrayed no signs of his uneasiness.

One evening as the old man sat quietly in his lodge, conversing with his wife and daughters, the patient looked up as if desirous of speaking.

"Speak, young man," said Mastwena, "our ears shall listen patiently to all you have to say."

The young man, encouraged by the words, said: "I am a Cree Indian, and my name is Pekan."

"Speak on, I am listening," said Mastwena, for the chief knew the Cree tongue and understood what the young man said.

Pekan continued: "Three weeks ago I left my home in the north and came south intending to steal some horses from the Blackfoot camp. When I reached the Blackfoot country I found the camps so well guarded that there was no chance of getting what I sought. I kept journeying southward in the hope of finding some camp unprotected, but was disappointed, and so made up my mind to return home. I laid myself down to rest, praying to my guardian spirit for protection and guidance. The sun had risen when I prepared to depart, and as I looked over the prairie, I saw three young men in the distance riding toward the south. When they had

ridden together for a little while I saw them get off
their horses and kneel down upon the ground. In
front of them was a large stone, and as I saw them
kneel and bow their heads, I knew that they were
praying to the gods. I watched them carefully, and
soon perceived that they were young men belonging
to the Blackfoot tribe. I dared not advance, for they
were well armed, so I contented myself with remaining in my place of safety, sheltered by some brush in
one of the coulees.

" As the young men were performing their devotions
a dark cloud passed over the sun, and strange noises
broke out in the air. They arose terror-stricken,
and attempted to flee, but found they were chained
to the spot. They beat their horses, but could not
make them stir. The cloud passed away, and then
they turned their horses' heads toward the north, to
return home; but an evil spirit had entered the
animals, and they fled toward the south. The young
men tried to throw themselves from their saddles,
but they were held firmly upon them by some demon
of the air. They prayed and cried for help, but no
good spirits came to their assistance. Horses and
riders rushed wildly into the country of the Crow,
Gros Ventres and Sioux Indians. I followed them in
haste, watching the frantic and useless efforts of the

young men to return. A band of Crow Indians out
hunting buffalo crossed their pathway, and as they
saw them madly riding, they gazed for a moment
with wild surprise, and then fled. The very animals
that roamed the prairies stood enchanted with the
wonderful vision, and forgot to flee. My heart beat
quickly as I followed them at a distance and watched
their mad flight.

"Onward they sped, half drunk with frenzy, riding
here and there among rocks, swamp and brush. Suddenly they returned and fell anew before the Stone of
Sacrifice, praying earnestly for help, and studying the
strangely written characters traced upon the rocks.
I desired strongly to go and warn them of their
danger, but was sore afraid.

"Ofttimes had I heard old chiefs tell of the misdeeds
of the prairie gods, their hatred toward the Indians,
and the terrible injuries they were able to inflict, and
I dreaded the results of this familiarity with the
spirit-book. Many years ago a Cree chief held intercourse with the spirits, and was able to do many
things that no other chief could do; but suddenly he
disappeared from the camp and no one ever afterward
learned where he had gone. These spirits are wonderful beings, flying where they will and doing what
they choose. I like not their company or friendship

When I remembered the strange things performed by
the spirits I trembled for the safety of the young men.
One of their number, giving his horse to one of his
comrades, advanced to the stone and traced with his
finger the wonderful writing which the spirits had
made thereon. Whilst thus engaged his whole body
was seized with trembling, weird voices were heard in
the air, the ground shook with a violent tremor, and a
feeling of helplessness took possession of the group.
Earth and air were alive with spirits, a grand assembly
apparently having taken place. The horses tried to
move, but the ground was enchanted, and the more
earnestly they strove to detach their feet from the
soil, the stronger were they held together.

"Suddenly the sky was lighted up with a bright
glow and the enchantment apparently was at an end.
The riders knelt upon the ground and prayed, and
then remounted and rode off leisurely southward. I
followed them at a distance, anxious to learn what
would be the result of this conference with the prairie
spirits and the visit to the Writing Stones. Hungry
and tired I sought rest and food among a clump of
berry bushes, intending to go on and see the end of
the vision—for such it seemed to me.

"How long I slept I do not know, so thoroughly
exhausted was I, but when I awoke the sun was

shining brightly and I felt refreshed. As I half reclined, rubbing my eyes, I was startled with the report of several guns at a short distance from me. Rising quietly and making my way through the brush, my knees smote each other and my heart sank within me as I heard a rustling sound. Looking up with gun in readiness for the approach of an enemy, I saw my horse galloping off. I had fastened him with a lariat to a small tree, but, startled by the report of the guns, he had broken loose, and was now making off so swiftly that I was unable to follow and recover him. There I was, afoot and in an enemy's country with strange Indians in the near distance. Arousing myself from the stupor into which I had fallen, I peered through an opening in the brushwood and beheld the three young men and their horses fallen to the ground. Six Indians, whom I perceived to be Gros Ventres, rode toward the place where they lay, and speedily dispatched them. Quickly dismounting they scalped them, and then rode away after having taken their guns. Evidently they had not perceived my runaway horse, for they came not to the place where I lay concealed.

"When I found that everything was quiet, I carefully followed the brushwood until I came near the spot where the bodies of the young men lay. They were still warm, but life was extinct. Covering them reverently and praying to the Great Spirit for his blessing, I turned my feet homeward, hoping that I might recover my lost horse. Four nights was I upon the road without any food and but little rest. Several times I fell to the ground and thought that I should die from sheer weakness, but after much pain and fatigue, I reached the top of the hill, from which I could easily see the curling smoke of your lodges. Life was of little consequence to me, so I made up my mind to come to this camp, knowing that you could not do any more than kill me: and here I am, and here, too, are the medicine bags belonging to the young men," saying which he handed Mastwena three medicine bags which the Gros Ventres had evidently overlooked in their hasty flight. These the old man at once recognized as belonging to the Blood Indians.

" Sad, sad was the day when the young men visited the Writing Stones," said Mastwena. " I have told the young men of our camps never to go there, as the spirits are angry with those who frequent their favored haunts, but they heed me not. Since I was a young man several of our people have gone there to consult these writings, and evil has always befallen our camps after one of these visits. I have felt afraid ever since I learned that the young men had gone

from the camp, and now my predictions have proved
to be true."

He bowed his head in silence, while the women
broke out into the death-wail, which soon spread
to the lodges of the relatives of the young men.
The young Cree Indian remained in the camp until
he was strong enough to go home, when the aged
Mastwena gave him a horse and food for the journey,
wishing him a safe return to the land of his people.

Many years have gone by since the young men
visited the Writing Stones, but whenever a hunting
party is going out from the southern lodges the aged
people relate the story of Mastwena and the Cree
youth, and the present generation shun the place
where the prairie spirits write upon the rocks, believ-
ing, as they do, that sorrow, pain, and death will
follow the unhappy transgressor who seeks to solve
the mysteries of the spirit world.

AKSPINE.

THOUGH known only by his Indian name, Akspine was one of the most genial, cultured Englishmen one could meet anywhere. He was born and educated in good old Yorkshire, trained in the faith of his fathers, and nursed by an honest and kind-hearted woman. As he grew into a fine, manly lad he attended the village school, was enthusiastic in his studies, full of energy and always ready to help a lame comrade or to seize any opportunity of doing good. If there was a widow or an orphan in the village, he was sure to devise some scheme to benefit that one, so that he soon became noted as a helper of the needy.

There was an old Mother Swann in the village who eked out a precarious living by taking in sewing. Yet her poverty did not seem to make the old lady unhappy: she always had a smile and a cheery word for every passer-by. A small patch of garden lay beside her cottage, but she knew of no one whom she could ask to dig it for her: her friends were far

11

away, and the acquaintances who lived near were as
poor and as fully occupied as herself. Every evening as she looked at it before retiring to rest she
wondered how to get her patch of ground made ready
for sowing. In this meditative mood she bent her
knee and thanked the Lord for all His goodness and
love, confessed her sins, prayed earnestly for a deeper
work of grace to be wrought in her heart, and pled
for a continuance of temporal blessings.

Wearied with toil at the close of a busy day, Mother
Swann was soon asleep, resting as only the honest poor
rest who trust in God and are content. The old
woman was grateful for the mercies given her, and
not covetous of those withheld and granted to her
more prosperous neighbors.

The birds were singing merrily in the early morning when she awoke. With a hymn of praise upon
her lips she arose and dressed, read a chapter in the
old Book, and spent a short time in silent devotion.
Drawing the curtain aside from the window and looking out she was surprised to see that a large portion
of her garden plot had been dug during the night.
Whether it had been done by the hand of man or of
angel she knew not, but it was a glad surprise, and
a source of bewilderment as well to the old woman.
Every morning for a week she saw the work progress

until it was finished, but without discovering who
were the busy toilers. Some weeks afterwards she
learned that a Workers' Club had been organized
at the village school for the purpose of helping poor
women and children. Zest for the work was given
by the feeling that it was done in secret. The lads
found that there was as much pleasure to be derived
from playing useful pranks as by foolish or cruel
ones. The promoter of this Workers' Club was
Akspine.

In a miner's shack in Montana a young man lay on
the floor, a group of miners and cowboys bending over
his inanimate body, rubbing and turning him over on
his face and using every means within their knowledge to restore life. For a long time their efforts
were unavailing: but, unwilling to give up, they continued while there remained a chance of success. At
length faint signs of returning animation revived
their hopes, and redoubling their efforts they were
at last rewarded by his recovery. The stranger
who had risked his life to save the child of one of
the settlers on the ranch from drowning had won
the hearts of the miners and cowboys by his brave
endeavor and pluck: hence no effort was too great
to make in order to restore him to life.

He had approached the river in the dusk of the evening and paused on the bank seeking a ford. As he sat his horse, gazing on the wildly rushing stream, seeing no spot which might be crossed in safety, and wondering what he should do, he heard a scream from the opposite shore, and saw a woman wringing her hands as she ran down to the river, crying, " My child! my child!"

To spring to the ground, throw off his coat and plunge into the turbulent stream was the work of a moment. The stranger struck out boldly toward the child as it was being carried away by the swift current. Keeping his eye on the tiny bundle, the courageous swimmer with almost superhuman effort made his way toward it, contending manfully with the force of the waters which barred his progress. The few settlers, attracted by the mother's cries, drew near the river and watched with breathless interest the battle for life. It was a terrible struggle, and the cowboys, as they ran along the bank with hair streaming in the wind, their hearts beating in alternate hope and fear, wondered whether the man or the river would gain the victory. Meanwhile the swimmer had reached the middle of the stream, and with a few powerful strokes overtook the precious bundle. Grasping it with a firm hold, he turned to the shore.

Anxious, praying hearts awaited him, and willing, but powerless, hands were stretched out to his aid. But the battle was not yet won; the force of the current carried him down, the terror-stricken mother following with her cries. He turned and turned again, at each attempt winning a few yards nearer the shore, but his strength was failing, though he still struggled bravely on. The weight of his now saturated clothes, as well as of the child, was dragging him under. Alas! was he to give his life for nought? Was he to perish and not save the child? Twice he sank, while the cries of the woman rent the air. Then as he arose once more to the surface, she sobbed, "Thank God!" Surely a kind Providence is watching over them and guiding the man among the jutting rocks and crags, saving him from being dashed upon the great boulders scattered along the bed of the river. Again he is nearing the shore, where men are waiting to grasp him. He sinks again. O God! Is it for the last time? No! A shout from the people, then one more brave effort! It is the last. He holds the child in his arms toward them, the men rush into the roaring waters and seize and bear both to the land.

The mother's arms received the babe. It is cold and apparently lifeless, but the women know what to do: they carry it away, apply restoratives, wrap

it in warm flannels and rub the little body until the
child breathes, smiles and opens its eyes to the
mother's anxious gaze.

The cowboys carried the stranger to the miner's
shack, and there by rough but kindly methods, and
with the determination not to desist while there
remained any hope, succeeded, as we have seen, in
restoring the brave hero to life.

One of the men recovered the horse left on the
other side of the river, and begged its owner to
remain among them. He thanked them for their
good-will and kindness, but declined, at the same
time refusing to take the reward offered him for so
risking his life.

As soon as the man was sufficiently recovered he
paid a visit to the humble shack of the settler to see
the child he had saved. As he took it in his arms it
smiled up into his face as though it too would thank
him for a rescued life. The father was profuse in
his gratitude, and the mother, with tears in her eyes,
tried to speak, but her heart was too full for words.
The stranger understood the language of her looks,
and valued such expression of her feeling better than
if it had been couched in the finest words ever spoken.
He bade the grateful parents farewell and rode away
with a glad heart, saying, " I have only done my

duty." There was no one in that settlement so happy as Akspine.

His career had been a chequered one since the days when he had organized and promoted the Workers' Club among his school-fellows. He had added an efficient musical training to his excellent English education. After serving an apprenticeship on one of the English railroads he married and went to India, where he became station-master on one of the lines. Owing to the ill-health of his wife he was obliged to give up that position at the end of two years and return to England. A few months later he followed her remains to the grave, and placing his infant daughter in the care of his wife's mother he emigrated to the New World, hoping in its new and stirring life to find solace for his sorrow, as well as remuneration for his toil. He had gone first to the home of a friend in the western States, where he remained a year. Later we find him the hero of this adventure on the river.

After leaving the settler's shack Akspine journeyed northward toward the international boundary line. On the way he encountered a camp of Indians, and being wearied with travel he stayed to rest, intending to remain with them only a few days.

The Indians' lodges were pitched in a beautifully

wooded valley. They had plenty of horses and
abundance of buffalo meat, and the weather being
cold he concluded to prolong his stay among them.
He employed his time teaching the Indians many
useful things, and before he left the camp at the end
of three months he had made many friends. He left
many specimens of his handiwork as memorials of
his stay with the natives of the Montana plains.
Oftentimes the Indians gathered in the Chief Peta's
lodge, where Akspine was a guest, to watch his busy
fingers carve dogs, horses, buffalo and moose from
blocks of wood with his knife.

One of the young men of the camp who watched
the white man most closely was Yellow Snake. He
was deeply interested in the work, asked that he
might learn the art, and proved an apt pupil. He
went out from the lodge and returned in a few days,
bringing an exact and perfect imitation of the work
done by Akspine. Between these two young men,
though representatives of different races, there sprang
up a deep attachment, and they became close companions. It was during his stay with these people
that Akspine received his Indian name, and this
brought him into still closer relationship with the
Indians.

There were sad hearts in the camp when at the

end of three months Akspine suddenly determined to
leave it and ride farther north. They had learned
to love him dearly, and had hoped to keep him
always with them: but Akspine could not stay, and
one fine morning he rode away into the enemy's
country. Scanning the horizon on all sides, and
keeping a sharp lookout for any sign of hostile
Indians, he had ridden five days' journey without
encountering a foe or meeting with any adventure.
He had slept on the prairie, picketing his horse near,
and using his saddle for a pillow. At the end of the
fifth day he drew near a wood which skirted one of
the rivers of the plains. Though appearances indi-
cated that he was not far from a white settlement,
he yet had to be as careful as though he were still
out on the lonely prairie. He first cared for and
secured his horse, and then, after eating his supper
of pemmican, lay down to rest at the foot of a sheltering tree, placing his gun and revolver close at hand,
for to lose either of them would be death: and he
could not be sure that a sudden emergency might
not arise when he should need them for self-defence.
The night was calm and clear, and with his thoughts
dwelling on the past and the home in the old land,
Akspine fell asleep. He was not far from the settlement of Mackleton, on the banks of the Marion

River, but was still within reach of any hostile Indians who might have an antipathy to the whites.

Akspine slept well until he was roused in the darkness of the early morning by the sharp report of a rifle. Grasping his gun he sprang to his feet, but could see no one. A second report rang out, followed by a groan. Turning in the direction from which the sound came, he heard a familiar voice utter his name, and recognized his friend Yellow Snake. From him he learned that two of the worst renegades in the camp had been heard plotting to slay him and steal his horse and other valuables. Yellow Snake had watched the men, and learning their destination had gone in another direction to the same spot. He had kept out of sight, yet knew where they were until he had seen Akspine enter the wood. Noting the place where the evil-disposed Indians had entered it, he had approached it at another. When Akspine lay down to rest he had crept up quietly and stationed himself near that he might keep guard and frustrate the wicked design of the would-be murderers. He knew by the movements of the Indians that they were likely to make the attack in the early dawn. His fears were fully realized. Long before the sun arose he made out two figures moving stealthily among the trees. Peering through the darkness he saw that each held his gun tightly in his hand. Yellow Snake watched them, and as they knelt down to take aim at the white man sleeping so peacefully at the foot of the tree, he raised his rifle and shot one of them dead; a second shot followed, and the other Indian fell to the ground with a groan. While Yellow Snake was relating all this to Akspine, a bullet whizzed past their ears. Grasping their guns they turned them upon the second Indian, whom they had thought dead. He was, however, only severely wounded, and had sufficient strength to raise his rifle and fire it. A bullet from Yellow Snake's gun finished him, and upon examination he found that the men were indeed two of the worst characters in the camp.

Akspine's gratitude was deep and sincere. He took Yellow Snake's hand in his and tried to stammer out his thanks in the little Indian language he had acquired while in the camp, but it was too slow and too inadequate a medium to express his feelings. He spoke from a full heart in his own English speech: "Yellow Snake, you have indeed been a true friend to me. Never can I repay you for your kindness and devotion. You have come a long way to protect me from these men, and if you had not done so I should have been killed. What can I do to pay you for it? Tell me and I will gladly do it."

Yellow Snake looked into Akspine's eyes as they shone with gratitude and love, and although he did not understand a word the white man had spoken, he gathered their import from his expression. A gleam of satisfaction was in his eyes and his face met Akspine's in its joy, as he answered in a few words:

"You are a stranger and a good man," he said; "I learned it from your life in our camp, and I love you as a brother. Let me go with you and I will be your companion and help you all I can. I have only done my duty."

Akspine and his friend carried the bodies of the slain Indians to the river bank, and fastening stones to the feet cast them in. They then spent some time searching for the horses that had belonged to the Indians, and when they found them, led them to the bank of the river and shot them there that the carcases might fall into the stream. Having disposed of all belonging to their foes, the friends crossed the river, and before setting out upon their day's journey, ate their morning meal with gratitude in their hearts to the Great Spirit for having preserved their lives.

The sun was high in the heavens before they were on their way northward, but by hard riding they reached a camp of the Blackfoot Indians before night fell. They found the lodge of Button Chief, who

received them kindly and treated them with his
accustomed hospitality, asking that they would make
his lodge their home. The travellers, being tired,
were allowed to rest, and although the news spread
rapidly among the lodges that a white stranger had
come to stay with them, and young and old were
eager to see him and learn the import of his visit, none
approached. Even the youngest showed no signs of
impatience. In such manner the Indians are taught
to suppress their emotions, and never to betray
surprise, joy or fear.

Upon the following day the chief gave a feast in
honor of his guests, and invited to it the other chiefs
and soldiers of the tribe. The crier stood outside the
lodge door and called them to come to the feast given
by the chief. The invitation met with a hearty
response, and a large party soon filled the lodge. The
choicest pieces of buffalo meat were placed before the
guests, and they were given an abundance of tea. The
pipes were filled again and again, and passed from
one to another of the company until they appeared
to be on fire, yet the pipes were filled again. When
these were smoked less vigorously the conversation
began in earnest.

An interpreter was found in the camp to repeat in
the ears of the people all that the white stranger had

to tell them. This man had spent some time among the whites, having been taken in hand to be educated by a merchant, but unable to remain away he had come back to find a home with his own people. He could understand all that Akspine said, and repeated it to the listening chiefs in their own tongue.

Akspine related many scenes of his life in the Old World, and astonished them beyond measure as he told of the wonders of the sea, and the mighty vessels which crossed the ocean and plied upon the rivers and lakes; of the large stone and iron buildings in the towns and cities: of the tens of thousands of people, and finally, of a visit to Windsor Castle. The "Great Mother" is to the natives of the north-western prairies the greatest among the chief men and women of the earth, a fact which is all the more singular when we remember the opinion generally held by the Indians on the inferiority of women. An aged warrior named White Calf had listened attentively, making no comment until Akspine told of the ships of iron manned by more than a hundred sailors and sailing across the ocean. Then he arose, and uttering a grunt of dissent and dissatisfaction, exclaimed:

"It is a lie! No one could do that. This white man is a medicine-man who has come to steal away the hearts of the people, and if you listen to him he will make you believe whatever he tells you." Saying which he departed, leaving the company doubtful whether to be amused or shocked.

The hours fled rapidly by as Akspine continued his wonderful tales of the white men and the strange land in which they dwelt. The interest increased as he related them, and though he was weary and would gladly have ceased, the intense eagerness of the Indians as they sat with eyes riveted upon him, drinking in his words with breathless excitement, made it impossible for him to refuse to gratify them. It was nearly midnight when they departed to their own lodges, and Akspine was permitted to retire. He had nothing to fear from the worst renegade in the camp, knowing that he was perfectly safe under the protection of the aged chief in whose lodge he dwelt. The Indians returned the following day, eager to hear more of the stories that had been related on the previous night. This continued for several nights, and there was yet no abatement of interest.

On the seventh night an unusually large company had assembled to hear Akspine recite the tales of the white men. The pipe was filled and passed around, then Button Chief turned to his guest and said :

"Tell us the story of the Master."

In a lower tone of voice than usual Akspine obeyed.

" Many years ago, when I was a boy, as I sat on the floor by my mother while she worked she told me of a time long past. It is a story of a company of men who bade farewell to their homes, their wives, children and friends, and went upon a journey across the sea. They hoped to make large sums of money there, and return to their native land to live in contentment all their days. The voyage was long, and the vessel that bore them did not return for two years. The captain of the ship then brought word that he had left his passengers in good health and excellent spirits, and the prospects of success on the island where he had landed them were good. Several years passed by and no word was received from any of the company. Intense anxiety was felt among their friends, and although many efforts were made to learn something of their fate, none were successful. All hope of ever hearing from them again had wellnigh passed away, the wives and mothers alone clinging to the belief that they would one day see or hear from their loved ones.

" In the early winter there came a rich stranger to the country from which the company of men had sailed so many years before. The stranger's home

was far distant, but he seemed to enter into and
sympathize heartily with all the schemes for the
welfare of the people of the land. As he went in
and out among them he soon learned of the long
absence of the adventurers. He talked to the women,
who were still sorrowing for their husbands and sons.
Day after day he listened to the story and sympathized with their grief. Often after he had been in
the houses of the poor, sums of money were found
where he had left them in order that they might be
used for the purpose of providing the needed food
and clothing.

" In the spring a large vessel came into the harbor.
The people flocked in numbers to see it, thinking it
might bring some intelligence of the lost ones, but it
brought no tidings. The sailors in the vessel had
been hired for a long voyage, and had brought her
around to take her owner on board from that port.
In a few days the stately stranger embarked. He
examined the machinery and general appointments of
the vessel, and when he had satisfied himself upon
her fitness for the expedition, he announced that
within a few hours they were to set sail for a distant
island.

" The moon was shining brightly as the fine ship
left the landing, the rich stranger standing on her

12

deck and looking kindly upon the large number of people who had come down to see him depart. In after years many of them remembered the kind words he had spoken to the women and children. A week later they learned that the ship had been built by the express order of the stranger, and the captain and crew engaged to go in search of the men who were supposed to have been lost so many years before. Love and sympathy had kept the stranger from making his purpose known. He had set about his important mission quietly that he might not arouse hope too soon in the people's minds, as well as to avoid the overwhelming expression of their gratitude which any hint of his intentions would certainly have excited. He was a man of few words and many deeds.

"Two years passed without any tidings of the stranger, when one day the whole town was awakened by the shouts of many voices from a vessel in the harbor. The people ran to the landing: hundreds were soon crowding one another to look on the band of aged men who stood together on the deck of the vessel. As she drew near the landing they scanned the faces of the passengers, and as one and then another recognized a friend or long-mourned loved one, a shout of joyous welcome rent the air. Men.

women and children rushed on the deck and threw
their arms around the necks of the old men, weeping
for joy as they repeated their names.

"So long absent, given up for dead and now restored
so suddenly and unexpectedly, the scene was one to
touch the heart of the hardest. The inhabitants of the
town wept as they saw the joy of the women and
heard their cries of 'Father!' 'Brother!' On that
morning the axe and spade were thrown aside, men
forgot to labor in the common joy. Few found time
to rest or eat as they gathered around the lost ones
that were found, and eagerly inquired the cause of
their long absence from home.

"They had reached their destination safely and
without delay had begun their labors. They were
hopeful and their hearts were light. Matters had
gone well with them for a year or two: then a
rebellion broke out in the land, they became impli-
cated, and it ended badly for them, the result being
that they suffered loss and were imprisoned for life.

"The long weary years which followed oppressed
their spirits, and losing all hope of ever returning to
their homes or their loved ones again, they longed for
death to release them from the heavy burden of
hopelessness and despair. Several of their number,
unable to endure, had sunk beneath the weight of

sorrow and the effects of the close confinement, and were borne to their last resting-place in a strange land, the sighs and groans of their comrades following them to the grave.

"But help was at hand, though they knew it not. One day a stately form entered the prison. With sympathetic countenance he inquired into their circumstances and listened to their story. A few days later the prison was again visited by the guard, who, bidding the remaining members of the party follow him, escorted them to a vessel lying in the harbor near. Soon the sails were set and they were homeward bound: but not until they were two days at sea did they learn the price that had been paid for their freedom.

"The stately stranger first offered the whole of his immense fortune for their release. This was refused, but when he added to the vast sum his own personal service, his sacrifice was accepted. Rather than leave the aged men to perish in prison in a strange land, he had sold himself into slavery, resolving to live and work as a slave in a foreign country that others might be free and return to their homes. The captain said the only message the stranger had given him to deliver were the words, 'Love one another!'

"The inhabitants of the town when they heard the

story told by the aged men, remembered the man who
had a smile and a kind word for everyone, the
stranger who had sailed his ship from their port to
the distant land. As the mothers and fathers sat
around their cottage hearths in the winter evenings,
happy in each other's presence, they related the story
of the man who had sold himself for them, and always
when they assembled in the morning or retired at
night they repeated the message, 'Love one another!'
When they spoke of him they called him 'Master,'
and seldom made mention of his name without
shedding tears of gratitude for his love."

Akspine's face shone as he continued his story, and
the eager listeners bent forward that they might catch
every word that fell from his lips.

"The Master," continued Akspine, " worked hard in
the service of the king, but he only lived for one year.
When he lay upon his death-bed and strangers gathered
around him, he closed his eyes ; then whispering softly
and tenderly the words, ' Love one another!' he gently
breathed his life away. The inhabitants of the town
for whose exiles he had given his life raised a magni-
ficent pillar to his memory, and inscribed upon its
base this simple phrase, and as the children gather
around it in the long summer evenings they repeat the
story of the Master, concluding ever with the words,
' Love one another!' "

As Akspine concluded his tale the Indians looked at each other and in hushed tones repeated the words, " Love one another !"

Deep thought was on every brow in that Indian lodge. Not a word was spoken. Each one arose, and gliding silently out went homeward thinking of the meaning of the simple message and the story of that wonderful life.

Night after night the lodge was filled with anxious listeners to hear again the story of the Master. Over and over again they said, " Tell us the story of the Master !" and as they repeated it to the women and children they said, " Wonderful ! Wonderful !"

Soon upon every lip and in every heart the sweet command, " Love one another !" was found. The noisy brawls formerly common to the camp ceased. The petty jealousies, the immorality, the love of war passed away before the influence of the gentle teaching of this tale among the red men. There was no longer cause for strife in the contemplation of this blessed life.

When their time came, and one and another of the aged men and women of the camps died, while friends gathered around their bed they looked up into the dusky faces and with their last breath whispered faintly, " Love one another !"

Akspine had not forgotten his music, and oftentimes sat in the lodges and played and sang sweet
songs to the chiefs and warriors while the people
gathered without to listen. His influence became very
great in the camps. He was initiated into some of the
secret societies and learned many of the mysterious
rites of the people. He entered heartily into their
schemes for improvement, and was always consulted
upon important questions, the chiefs recognizing the
power of his intellect, his courage and the purity of
his life.

He soon became thoroughly familiar with the
language of the tribe, and could converse in it upon
any subject. Young and old were strongly drawn to
him. He became as one of themselves, thinking
about the same things, engaging in the same kind of
work. It was impossible for him to remain long in
such intimate relationship to the people without form-
ing some attachment more sacred than others, though
he loved Yellow Snake as a brother and Yellow
Snake was always true to him.

The tribe was noted for its many beautiful maidens,
young women of gentle, pleasing manners, modest and
neat, and it was not possible that such should fail to
attract the notice of the white stranger. Dressed in
their native garb they were comely and attractive, and

some of them slyly added a little more paint to their faces or a few more ornaments to their hair when they knew they were likely to pass the lodge where Akspine dwelt.

In this lodge there was a lovely maiden of fourteen winters, who sat entranced for hours while Akspine played on his flute, or sang the plaintive songs of his native land, or who listened absorbed while he repeated the oft-told tales to the wondering natives. The maiden hung upon his words as a true worshipper, yet she never spoke to him nor showed by look or act that his words conveyed any meaning to her ears. She was only one of her father's chattels, to be disposed of as he wished. True, her father loved her, but she was only a girl, and in the Indian camp that meant in value a few horses, more or less, according to her good looks.

Unconsciously she trimmed her long black hair neatly, painted her face and the parting of the hair, arranged the necklace of bear's claws about her graceful throat, or the rings on her fingers, the bracelets of brass wire on her wrists, and the pretty beaded moccasins on her tiny feet. Her dress was made of the antelope skin well dressed and white, fashioned as a wide-flowing gown with two holes for sleeves, the top and bottom neatly trimmed with the teeth of the antelope and bear. A wide belt, to which was attached a piece of steel procured by the Indians from the traders, was fastened about her waist. Her limbs from the knees downward were clothed in a pair of beautifully embroidered leggings. Natoatchistaki, or the Rabbit woman, the daughter of Button Chief, was one of the beauties of the Indian camp. Every morning she went to the river and performed her ablutions. In the summer she swam across the swiftly flowing stream, and sported in the waters as if in her native element.

Akspine looked upon the maiden with the dark hair and eyes, but said no word of love to her; he was silent, though his heart bade him speak. The old chief beheld with satisfaction that the white stranger was suffering: he knew well what caused the failing appetite, the listless action and unrest.

It is customary among the Indians for the father of the young man who desires a wife to negotiate with the father of the maiden, and for a certain valuation, averaging from two to eight or ten horses, to be placed upon her. After these negotiations are completed the sale or marriage is ended by a season of festivities.

Akspine had no wealth and no friend to make arrangements for him, yet he was anxious to obtain

the maiden for his wife. The chief watched Akspine
with a loving eye, and seeing his wish, said : " My
friend, you are a stranger among us. You have
endeared yourself to us by your words and actions,
and we have learned to love you. You have healed
our sick people and taught the children. Since you
have come among us my people have been more contented and happy than they have been for years. We
cannot repay you for the kindness and courage you
have always shown, and although we belong to a
different race we can see that the hearts of all men
are the same. The Great Spirit made us all. We
now wish you to become one of ourselves. You have
learned our language and know some of the customs
and mysteries of our religion and our secret societies,
but we wish you to forget your own people and live
always with us, to make your home here and claim
us as your people. We cannot give you much ; we
cannot tell you of wonderful things or show you
such great works as you have seen among your own
people, but we have glorious records of brave men,
heroes who belong to us and who for the love they
bore their country and their people laid down their
lives with their faces to the foe, singing their death-
songs as they saw death approaching.

" We have decided in the council of the chiefs that

the bravest should give you the daughter he loves best for a wife. There is not one in the camp too good for you. I now offer you my daughter Natoat-chistaki. Take her and let her build you a lodge where you may dwell in peace. My heart is sad in losing her, for I love her above all the others, but I shall go often to your lodge and there I shall talk with you. Take her. She is yours. That is all I have to say."

As the chief finished, Akspine raised his head and let it fall in token of acquiescence in the decision, then the brave old man arose and left his lodge. His heart was full, but he would not allow his emotions to control him. He walked away dignified and silent, and no one meeting him could have told from his manner that anything unusual had occurred.

When Akspine looked up the lodge was empty. He remained alone in deep meditation, pondering over the step which was to sever him from his kindred and unite him forever with the Indians of the plains. He felt compelled to listen to the eloquence of his heart, and after a short struggle he decided to obey its dictates.

This decision made, and his heart lightened of the burden of doubt, Akspine went out into the adjoining bluffs where he could listen to the songs

of the birds and gather courage to meet the new
life. Darkness had fallen before he returned to the
lodge. When he sought his accustomed place, the
other occupants turned their eyes on him, but no
word was spoken. Four days passed, during which
no reference was made to the conversation that had
taken place, but on the fifth evening a merry group
assembled in the chief's lodge. The women in the
camp had prepared many dainties; the best food was
provided, venison and buffalo tongues were freely
given, and the guests ate eagerly of the good things.
It was a marriage feast indeed. Amid the rejoicing
and feasting many gifts were bestowed; then the
young men and maidens gathered outside the lodge as
the bride and bridegroom were escorted from the
home of the old chief to a lodge that had been lately
built and handsomely furnished. Here, after many
expressions of good-will, the company separated, each
retracing his steps to his own lodge.

Thus were Akspine and Natoatchistaki married in
the Indian fashion, their courtship coming after marriage, a reversal of the method of the white men. In
many cases the plan works well, but in the instances
where no courtship follows, there is bitter enmity,
slavery, and at last rejection. Akspine and his Indian
bride, however, loved each other devotedly, and were
happy.

After the first few days had lapsed, their friends came to call upon them in their own lodge. As the days passed the influence of the white man increased, though some of the young men were jealous of the power he wielded over the tribe. Within a short time he had attained the highest position and been made a chief. While sitting in the council of the chiefs Akspine listened attentively, offered no advice, but waited until all the others had spoken, then in a few clear, decisive words he unravelled the difficulty, showing by his ability to settle knotty questions that he was possessed of superior wisdom. His fame spread rapidly beyond his own tribe, and many Indians belonging to other camps were anxious to see him, but he was guarded closely by his people lest harm should come to him or an enemy attack him.

The power of the tribe grew. When drawn into war they conquered, but the wise counsels of Akspine enabled them often to avert it without losing honor among the nations. Peace and contentment reigned in the camps, the herds of horses multiplied, and the health of the people was good.

With a grave and dignified air the white chief strode through the camp, calling at a favorite lodge here and there to consult with the wise men on matters affecting the welfare of the tribe. At such times the children ran to him for the kind word or smile that was always ready for them.

Akspine's lodge became the resort of all who were in trouble. The sick sought his advice, the chiefs came to consult him, the young men resorted to him for encouragement, and when domestic troubles divided members of the same family, it was to Akspine's lodge they came to have the difficulty settled and the wounds healed. The young chief's wise rule indeed rested like a benediction upon all classes. Wherever he went, peace followed his footsteps. Several years were spent in thus influencing others for good, and the white chief was happy in the possession of such power over the people.

Early one morning during the fall of the year Akspine started on a trip to the mountains, accompanied by one of his friends, expecting to be absent four or five days. He chatted freely with his companion as he passed the lodges on his way through the camps, giving a word of counsel here and a gentle reproof there. The people smiled as he greeted them at the doors of the lodges, and prayed for success in his enterprise in the mountains.

Five days passed quickly, but Akspine did not return. No fears, though, were entertained for his

safety, but when two more days had come and gone
without bringing tidings of him, the people grew
anxious, and runners were sent to discover the cause
of his prolonged absence. Day after day the search
was continued, but without success.

All hope of learning anything of their beloved chief
had well-nigh fled from the hearts of the people when
suddenly the wail for the dead fell upon their ears.
The women rushed from the lodges and looked in the
direction from which the sound came. A travaille
drawn by a single horse was seen approaching slowly,
led by two young men, who bowed their heads as they
uttered the sad wail.

The foremost of the young men was Yellow Snake,
the bosom friend of Akspine. Faithful to the last, he
had not given up the search for his friend until he
had tracked the footprints of his horse to a crossing
that was deep and treacherous. Here the footprints
had ended, but Yellow Snake followed the stream, still
searching, until it entered a lake. Straightway he
plunged into the clear water, and after diving many
times he at last found the remains of Akspine and his
companion. He brought the bodies to the shore and
left them until he procured a travaille on which to
convey them to the camp.

Men, women and children gathered around the

travaille, weeping bitterly.   They carried Akspine to his lodge, wrapped him in his chief's garments, and then in solemn state they bore him to a lofty eminence beyond the camp.   On this height a warrior's lodge was built, and the body of the great white chief, Akspine, was placed within it.   He was surrounded by all the insignia of his office and securely guarded by his people's love.   There at the close of day the women gathered to mourn, and as they lifted their faces heavenward, reiterated in the plaintive cadences of grief the cry, "Akspine! Akspine!"

Many years have gone by, yet on the hill young and old meet at eventide to repeat the story of the white chief who told them of the Master and taught them always to say, "Love one another!"

OLD GLAD.

CHAPTER I.

SMALL company of men were sitting about a camp-fire on the prairie, enjoying their pipes and chatting. They were all trappers and traders. Their deerskin coats, with embroidered bands and fringed shoulders, were tanned soft, and soiled from constant wear. The beaded leggings generally worn by the half-breeds were replaced by long boots that reached to the knee; their cartridge belts were well filled, the stocks of their revolvers bright, and the knife stuck in the beaded or leathern sheath was sharp and keen.

The men were typical specimens of the class of hardy, honest, true-hearted hunters, who held a proprietary right over the prairies second only to those of the aboriginal possessors. Having no newspapers, and but few letters or correspondence with the more civilized world, and therefore scant means of obtaining news of events which serve as topics of conversation to men nearer the centres of civilization, they

13

talked of old times, repeated stories they had heard, or recounted the adventures and experiences that had fallen into their own lives or surroundings.

Long practice in the art of story-telling had made some of them excellent *raconteurs*, and though the style and diction in which the stories were couched might not bear criticism from the standpoint of literary perfection, they had the charm of being personal recollections, veritable history, and also of being told in the vernacular most intelligible to the listeners.

" Wall, boys, I've been down to bed-rock many a time, but you bet I never came so near givin' in my checks as in the year of the big snow. It wus the worst year for cold and sickness we ever had in the country."

The speaker was Old Glad, the famous hunter and trapper. Several of the men, with their long unkempt hair, presented a wild appearance, but the speaker had a soft, sweet voice and a mild expression of face. This gentle tone gave a dignity to the peculiar phraseology of the West. Old Glad had come as a lad from the shores of the St. Lawrence, and had been for several years in the employ of the Hudson's Bay Company.

Following the custom of that honorable corporation

he had taken to wife one of the Indian women of the Cree tribe, and had been happy and content with her. He had a number of sons and daughters who were no small comfort and help to their mother during his absence on buffalo hunts or while working at the different trading posts in the country.

Old Glad was a favorite among his comrades, and they leaned forward that night by the fire to listen to his tale of the by-gone days.

"In my old shanty up in the mountains, I wus tryin' to live through the hard times, huntin' some bear an' deer, an' eatin' whatever I could get. The snow wus deep an' it wus terrible cold, but I ses to the old woman, 'There's no use grumblin', fur that won't bring in buffalo meat.' We hed a few sacks of pemmican an' berries, but that couldn't last long with so many mouths to fill.

"Wall, late one night, an' it *wus bitter* cold, I heard the door open, an' lookin' up from the fire I saw a white man come in. He wus half naked, an' I didn't like his looks; he had a kind o' skeered look about him that wasn't much in his favor. But I couldn't turn him out on such a cold night, so I giv' him a seat by the fire an' my woman made him some supper.

"He had little to say, and the poor dog eat what

wus made for him as if he had been starved fur a
whole month.   He stayed with us fur three or four
weeks, an' it wur while he wus with us, one o' my
wee uns took sick.   She wur the best o' the house,
an' we grudged losin' her.   The stranger 'd come to
her hammock an' sit down an' begin to coo to her, an'
the wee un 'd open her eyes an' a bit of a smile wud
come to her face.

"Arter a while he wud sing to her—some queer
songs they wur—an' the wee un wud try to follow
him, though she wur so sick she couldn't hold up her
head.   Wall, she kept gettin' worse, an' I made up
my mind there wus no chance fur her.

"Some years afore, one o' my little folks wur sick
just like wee Nan, an' a doctor come along our way
an' gave us some medicine that cured him : an' he
wrote a perscription on a piece o' paper an' told us if
any o' the children wus taken sick again, if we sent
to Bennivale, where he lived, if he couldn't come
himself, he would send medicine to help us.

"Wall, this night I walked up an' down wishin' I
could go, but I couldn't leave my folk, an' it wus
blowin' an' snowin' so as no man could ha' found his
way to Bennivale.   It wur on the Missouri River,
more'n two hundred miles away.

"I looked at the paper over an' over again, an'
wished I could go.   I wus walkin' an' lookin' at wee

Nan an' then at my woman, an' then at the stranger. He said his name wus Bill, and that wus all I could get from him, so I sometimes called him 'Prairie Bill' an' sometimes 'Wanderin' Willie.'

"Wall, I sat down in the old chair, an' I saw Bill lookin' at wee Nan very serious like, an', wud you believe it, comrades, there wus tears in his eyes.

"That night I wus gettin' some wood fur the fire when I saw Bill ridin' off on his horse, an' I thought he'd got tired an' wus goin' to some o' the shanties in the mountains, 'r mebbe to the Indian camp. I thought it queer he should go away in that fashion an' never tell me where he wus goin', but of course it wus none o' my business, so I said nothin'.

"Wall, the storm got worse, and wee Nan didn't get any better. I sat beside her night after night, an' the wee thing kept singin' the songs Bill had been singin'. It wus queer, fur though she wus very sick, she would keep cooin' like Bill, an' then she wud close her eyes an' keep dosin'.

"We tried the medicines the Indians gave us, but they didn't do her no good. Often I wished the storm would stop, and I near made up my mind a dozen times that I'd go to Bennivale an' see the doctor anyway.

"The days an' nights went by slow, an' as I wus sittin' by the little un the door opened an' in come Bill, an' without sayin' a word, jest as if he'd gone out o' the door an' come right back, he put his hand in his pocket, an' pulls out a parcel o' powders an' giv' them to me. It was the doctor's writin', an' I knew it. He put a letter along with the medicine, an' this is what he said, fur I always carries this letter with me wherever I go:

" ' Dear Mr. Glad '—ye see, he called me by my old name o' the mountains, which I like best, fur it keeps me in mind o' the prairies an' the foot-hills. I can't speak it in the fine style he writes in, but I'll read it like our talk o' the prairie.

" Here's what he ses: 'Dear Mr. Glad, a stranger named Bill has just returned sufferin' with exposure, an' he has just informed me that one o' your children is very sick—a little girl. From all the fac's o' the case, which I wus able to gather from yer friend, I am able to send you some medicine which I feel sure will restore her. Mix the powders accordin' to directions. Whenever you come this way, bring me a few furs, and I will pay you fur them. I want some good beaver skins. Your friend Bill is a rare chap. He has had an excellent edication, and has seen better days. You can't go wrong in trustin' that fellow. He is sharp, clever an' queer.

" ' Sincerely yours,

" ' Tom. Ketson, M.D.'

"Comrades, as I read the letter I looked up an' saw that Bill wus pretty sick. He had suffered pretty bad from cold an' hunger, an' was a good deal frost-bitten.

"It wasn't long afore we fixed the powders for wee Nan, an' got Bill in good shape, but he wus very bad.

"Wall, the wee thing began to mend, an' Bill, lyin' beside the fire, though he couldn't speak much fur pain, wud sing a wee song, and coo to her—the stranger an' the wee un wur like lovers, an' they both kep' gettin' better.

"After a time wee Nan got round again, but Bill never got over his long ride, fur it left a bad cough that settled on his lungs, an' he lost half o' one foot an' some toes off the other.

"Wall, last summer I went back to the old shanty where I used to live, to fix the fence round Nan's grave, fur ye remember, comrades, that she left us three years ago, an' we buried her beside the shanty. As I wus fixin' the fence, I saw a man walkin' with two sticks, an' he wus comin' to the shanty. I wus a wee bit suspicious, an' I stepped aside into the bush to see if he wur after mischief. He come up to the grave, an' kneeled down beside it, an' then he took some flowers—roses an' the like—an' planted them on the grave. I waited fur a long time till I saw him wander off, an' then I come down an' finished my job.

"I saw him go to one of the coulees, an' there I found his shanty. I dropt in to get somethin' to eat, just fur an excuse, an' when the door wus opened it wus Bill 't met me.

"Boys, ye mind that cripple that ye wus laughin' at in camp the other day? Wall, he's passed in his checks. Ye won't trouble him any more. I went to dig his grave, an' I made the best coffin I could fur him. The boys made fun o' him because he wus only a cripple an' he wus poor. They called him 'Tanglefoot Bill,' an' a good deal o' sport they got out o' him. Wall, when I looked at his feet an' heard him cough, I thought o' the day I wus mendin' the grave an' of the stranger who went fur the medicine fur wee Nan.

"I put a board at the head o' the poor feller's grave, an' these is the words I wrote on it:

> "'To the Memory o' Prairie Bill,
> the Friend o' wee Nan.'"

When Old Glad had finished his story the men knocked the ashes out of their pipes, and wrapping themselves in blanket or skin, turned over on the sod and went to sleep. They had to make an early start in the morning, and though they made no comment they felt no interest in asking for another story that night.

After breakfast no time was lost: the dishes were washed, and the " boss " of the outfit put everything in order to start the long cavalcade of men and horses. Three heavily laden wagons were fastened to each other, and then ten or twelve horses hitched together to draw the load. Four or five of these teams comprised a train, and the manager of the whole was the " wagon-boss." He was generally a shrewd, hard-working, capable man. Black Jack was the name by which the boss of the train to which Old Glad was attached was known. He was a sterling fellow, big and strong, with long hair and heavy moustache. He was a man of few words, but an excellent boss-captain of the fleet of prairie schooners. Though many of the men he employed on his fleet were accustomed to use pretty strong language while on the trips across the prairie, they desisted when with Black Jack. He was a stern man, but with his stern determination had a kindly manner and a love of honesty which affected his men and imbued them with something of the same spirit that animated him.

Jack had married a handsome half-breed woman, who lived in a neat log shanty in one of the settlements that had grown up around the Hudson's Bay posts. She was queen of the home, and her chief

pride lay in having it well kept and attractive to
her husband when he returned from the long. trips
on the prairie. The house was a small one, but ample
for their needs. It was built of hewn logs laid one
above the other until the walls were about eight feet
high. Notched ridge-poles formed the roof, which
was thatched with prairie hay and moss and made
water-tight by a plastering of mud. The interior had
white calico stretched over the ceiling and was white-
washed with lime. The walls were covered with
pictures from the illustrated papers, which served the
double purpose of keeping out the wind and providing a sort of universal library and reading room,
affording many hours of amusement to Julia and her
friends.

Two years previous to his marriage a little girl in
the settlement had been left an orphan. Jack had
taken compassion on her and provided her a home,
and Alice was now the joy of his household. He
spent many of his leisure hours in making her toys.
She was a pretty, dimpled-cheeked child with light
hair and blue eyes, and was always happy and strong.
The Indians called her Curly Hair, but Jack had
named her Alice. While he guided the long train of
wagons across the prairie the wagon-boss's thoughts
were often in the log house with his little girl.

Black Jack had therefore been one of the most interested listeners to Old Glad's story of wee Nan and Prairie Bill.

A halt was called at noon, and after a spell of rest they journeyed onward steadily, until as darkness fell they entered the trading-post of Whoop Up.

After picketing their horses and wagons inside the stockade they had supper, and sat down around the fire to talk. The manager of the Fort had much to ask of Black Jack and his men concerning the prospects of the buffalo trade, the condition of the Indians and the probabilities of the weather, and then they drifted into the old course of story-telling.

A few minor anecdotes were told and enjoyed, but when Black Jack looked up from the fire and spoke his men listened eagerly.

"Our visit here," he said, "reminds me of the year of the small-pox among the Indians."

The wagon-boss spoke excellent English, and in spite of the many years spent on the prairie he had retained much of the purity of his native speech.

"It was very late in that fatal year. The Bloods, Blackfeet and Piegans were restless and seemed bent on war, and the Crees and Assiniboines were none the less fidgety. Not far from here, on the banks of the Belly River, a band of Bloods and Blackfeet were camped, and the South Piegans had pitched their tents on the St. Mary's River.

"The Crees and Assiniboines, as you know, hate the Blackfeet. There is a tradition that many years ago when the Crees and the Blackfeet were united as one family, there was only one dog in the camp, and some of the people having quarrelled over the possession of this animal, the tribes took up the quarrel and soon were at enmity, and although they have made treaties of peace since there never has been the same unity as existed in former years.

"They were at the time of my story bitter enemies to each other, and the Crees thought they could do no better than take advantage of the great loss sustained by the Blackfeet and Bloods through the ravages of the small-pox plague and attack them. They had, therefore, come down to the Little Bow country with this determination, and encamping there waited for accurate information as to the strength and location of their enemies.

"The Bloods, Blackfeet and Piegans were well armed, having obtained good rifles from the traders across the line, but the Crees and their confederates had nothing but arrows and old guns supplied them by the Hudson's Bay Company.

"The Crees sent forward a band of seven or eight

hundred warriors to reconnoitre. These came upon
a band of Blood Indians camped near the Fort and
attacked them, killing a few men and women.

"This roused the camp, and it did not take long to
send word to the Blackfeet and Piegans. The Bloods
had lost some of their best men and were in the mood
to fight desperately.

"In the early morning the fight began in earnest.
The Bloods assisted by their allies drove the Crees
hard. Overcome by superior numbers they were forced
to retreat lower down the river until they reached the
big coulees where the trail crosses the river.

"You remember the big coulees beside the trail;
but it was a little lower down the Belly River that the
battle raged the hottest. The Crees and the Assiniboines were in one coulee, the Piegans in another, and
the Blackfeet and Bloods in a third.

"Well, boys, I believe that was one of the greatest
battles ever read of, for the fellows fought like
troopers. Talk about your British soldiers, there are
none living who could beat some of those men for
courage and skill according to their own methods.

"The Crees put their horses down in one of the
river bottoms to shelter them from the bullets of the
foe, and although they had no better weapons than
bows and arrows and old guns, they had the advantage

of their enemies in position. They fought desperately for some hours, however, without gaining much on either side. As they were unable to reach each other and engage in a hand-to-hand fight, nor to learn the actual strength of the enemy, they were too wise to risk an open attack. As they lay hidden by the ridge of the coulee they crawled to the top and fired. Some of the Crees, more daring than the others, raised themselves above the edge and were immediately shot down by their enemies. The better weapons of the Blackfeet were telling, and the Crees were getting the worst of the fight. Seeing this they determined by a sudden movement to evade the Piegans and Blackfeet. They rushed down the coulee, sprang on their horses and made for the river. The Piegans saw them and pursued them, and a general fight followed, in which both Piegans and Crees were carried over one of the steep precipices. Some were killed outright, others badly injured. Stones were hurled into the ravine by those above, bruising the warriors of both sides.

"Still the Crees and Assiniboines dashed into the river. Many of them were shot or carried down by the current. The Bloods and Blackfeet went in after them and a terrible slaughter took place. As the Crees struggled in the water they were shot down like dogs.

"It was terrible to slay the poor creatures in such a cruel fashion, but an old Indian friend of mine who was at the fight told me with glee that it was splendid sport, for if the Crees had got the chance they would have done the same thing to them.

"Others of the Blackfeet crossed the river higher up and engaged the Crees in another skirmish, in which about fifty were killed.

"If you go along the river now I can show you some of the piles of stones that were raised to mark the spot where Blackfeet and Bloods fell, and others where the Crees were slain. A great many of the latter were killed, but we never learned the exact number, so many were carried down the river.

"My old friend Jerry Potts said the Blackfeet only lost about fifty.

"The tribes had, however, apparently enough of fighting, for the very next year they made a treaty, and have never since gone to war with each other. Since the white men came to the country they seem to think they have a common enemy and no time to fight among themselves."

When the boss had finished his story the men spread their buffalo robes and blankets on the floor, and lay down on them to sleep the sound sleep that only an open-air life can induce.

CHAPTER II.

Up among the foot-hills of the Rockies, far from
the villages that have sprung up in the western
country, nestling beneath the shadow of the everlast-
ing hills, a tiny cottage shanty stands. The way to it
from the main trail is hidden behind the overlapping
spurs of hill which rise in undulating lines from the
plains to the bewildering passes of the mountain
range. The sun alone seems to have found its way
to it, and shining down in a benediction of beauty
brings its picturesque outline into bold relief against
the background of sun-kissed cloud and sheltered
mountain tops.

Some anchorite surely, weary of the world, whose
wounded spirit needs the healing influences of nature
unalloyed by man, has built his dwelling here. Some
artist who would saturate his senses with the beauty
of the ever-changing shadows, the luxury of color,
the softness of the veiling mists, the tender touch of
coming night, the mystery of distance, has come here.

How refined must be the nature of the occupant of
such a spot! How attuned his life to nature's moods!
Alas! How long will the place be unspoiled by man?
How long before the aggressive enterprise of the
commercial spirit of the age will send its locomotive

to insult the clouds with its nether smoke and the disturbing sounds of hurrying traffic ?

The early summer had passed, the days had begun their downward course, and the nights were colder. A traveller who had come to the Rockies in search of better air and health had wandered many miles from the village where he had taken up quarters for the season. The many and beautiful flowers which grow in rich profusion among the foot-hills had attracted his steps and robbed his limbs of all sense of fatigue. He was all unconscious of the distance he had walked or how far he was from the village. He was drinking in health with every breath of the pure mountain air, beauty with every bud or blossom he gathered, and such things as supper or bed were of a secondary nature to him at the moment.

As he stooped to pick yet another flower more perfect than the last, he was accosted with the words, "Good-day, Stranger !" spoken in a soft minor key. Turning, he saw an old grey-haired man. There were lines of care and thought in the face, yet not such as have been furrowed deep by rebellion against the discipline of life. His dress was that of an old-timer of the mountains, its buckskin in picturesque harmony with the surroundings.

The traveller having responded courteously to the

14

greeting, the two men were soon deep in a pleasant conversation.

"This is a delightful country: the air is so pure and the scenery grand," said the stranger, by way of preface.

"Yes; a man must get a long way off nowadays to think and breathe," was the unexpected reply.

"Do you live in this part of the country?"

"Yes, I hev' a shanty in the hills, an' if ye'd care to look in I'll give ye a welcome. We're a bit rough in these parts, for we don't see strangers often, an' we're willin' to just live in our own way an' be content," and turning the old man led the way up the winding path in the hills.

Each bend and higher level reached revealed fresh beauty to the eye of the stranger, and when their steps crossed a wimpling, bubbling mountain stream to the shanty he had seen from the distance, words failed him to express his appreciation of the beauty of the spot.

"Lovely!" Far away the forest-crowned mountain tops pierced the clouds and hid from sight the snows and glaciered sides. Bright rivers wound about the foot-hills or plunged into the great canyons and were lost to sight. The stranger stood entranced, as if caught in some vision beyond his power to grasp the meaning of, and the mountaineer, knowing well the feeling, waited silent by his side.

Later, when seated before the door of the shanty they watched the sun go down, a sight to be remembered for all time, the hearts of the two men were one in praise to the Great Creator of the universe, the Master-mind who had so clothed the land with beauty and given to the mind of man the capacity to enjoy it.

Old Glad's quaintly ' proffered hospitality was willingly and gratefully accepted, and after his guest had been refreshed by a nicely cooked supper, their talk turned to the past in the old mountaineer's life. The story-telling days of camp and prairie were once more revived.

"Have you always lived up here in the mountains?"

" No, but I hev bin here most of my life. Ye see there's not much to annoy ye here, an' I don't keer fur all yer noise in the towns. There's nothin' like the prairie an' the mountains fur a man to get a livin' in an' be happy."

"And have you always found the happiness you wished for in these places?" asked the stranger with interest. "Happiness is what I have ever been in quest of, and I must confess I have failed to find what I desired."

"Wall, I've got along pretty well. Of course I've had my hard times like other folk an' been down to bed-rock many a time."

"Have you all your children with you?"

"No. I've lost some, like my neighbors. It's not so very long since we buried Nan, and then my Bill went like all the rest." And the old man sighed as he paused for a moment. The stranger waited until he spoke again.

"Yes, Bill was a brave lad. He was born in the Indian camp when I wus workin' fur the Company, away in the north. The little fellow ran among the lodges, an' it wusn't long till he could talk Cree, an' Blackfoot, an' Sioux, an' French. He wus a good rider an' a fine hand at the gun. I tell ye I wus proud o' him when he wus a little fellow. The Indians an' half-breeds wus afeard o' him, 'cause, ye see, he could ride an' shoot better'n them, an' he wus a fine talker in the Indian camps. I min' once when he wus a little fellow runnin' around the Fort an' up to all kinds o' tricks, that he went off with Long Tom the half-breed, without lettin' me know.

"Tom wus a good shot, but a reckless fellow, an' if ye didn't look out he wus sure to get hinself an' his friends into trouble. After he had gone some o' my comrades come an' told me, an' I wusn't well pleased, but I thought it 'ud turn out all right, so I said nothin', an' waited fur him to get back.

"Wall, ten days went by an' I wus gettin' kind o' anxious, an' I made up my mind if he didn't get back in a couple o' days I'd go off an' look fur him.

"Late that night as I wus sittin' by the fire he come in. The wee fellow had his head tied up with a bit o' blanket, an' one o' his arms in a sling. His moccasins wur worn off his feet an' he couldn't speak. He looked in my face an' kin' o' staggered an' fell down on the floor. He wur completely done. I jumped out o' my old cheer an' took him in my arms. His head wus badly cut an' his hair all stickin' wi' blood, an' his arm wus bruised an' black. We got him fixed up in bed an' didn't ask any questions fur two weeks. Then he told his story. Long Tom an' him had gone off to shoot deer an' weren't havin' much success, an' when their grub wus all gone an' they had to live on berries, they thought they'd better get back.

"As they wur sittin' down restin' a bit an' their horses wur feedin' they heard a terrible rush, an' lookin' up saw their horses racin' toward them an' a grizzly standin' kind o' meditatin'. Long Tom up with his gun an' fired, but missed his aim, an' wud

ye believe it, his horse fell dead, shot through the
heart. The grizzly jumped on him and threw him to
the ground. My wee fellow ran back a few paces
an' took aim. He sent two bullets into the b'ar, but
the old fellow was hard to die. He left Tom an' made
fur the boy. But he just made one spring and struck
Bill down 'fore he giv' his yell an' fell dead.

"The poor boy lay on the ground, his head covered
with blood an' his arm bruised where the b'ar had
struck him. Long Tom couldn't move, an' by an' by
the lad, who was a plucky un, crawled over to him.
He saw he wus bad, an' at first he didn't know what
to do. They had only one horse, an' Tom couldn't
walk, an' thur wurn't a post fur miles.

"Wall, they lay there fur a while an' then Tom
got a bit better an' my lad put him on the horse an'
started fur home. Bill wanted fur to take the
grizzly's skin, but they wur too done to get it, so
they hed to leave it. My Bill walked alongside the
horse an' got berries fur Tom an' him to eat, fur they
hed no grub. It wur two days 'fore they got to the
Fort an' my Bill had left Tom at his shanty.

"I tell ye, it wur a close shave, an' it wus a long
time 'fore the lad wur strong again, but as soon as he
wur able to climb on his horse again he wus off
out shootin' an' huntin'."

"He must have been a brave lad."

"Ay, he wur that, stranger, as brave a lad as ever lived among these mountains."

"I should like to meet him some day and have a talk with him."

"Ah, stranger, he hev passed in his checks, an' we'll not see him again!" and the soft voice was sad and the buckskin sleeve was brushed hastily across the old man's eyes, brave in his grief as the lad had been in his encounter with the terrible grizzly.

Many stories are told of the pluck and bravery of this son of our old friend Old Glad. He had grown to man's estate, had married a Cree Indian woman and was settled down as an interpreter in the employ of the white men in the country.

One night when he had just returned from a long, wearisome trip over the prairies with a party of travellers, he was awakened about midnight by an Indian woman tapping at his shanty window. He sprang to his feet and listened; in a moment he heard the sound of the tramp of a band of horses. He roused a few of the settlers in the vicinity of his shanty, and they started in pursuit of the stampede. The men in advance with the horses heard the party coming behind and increased their speed. Not a word was uttered, but with the lariats they lashed their horses and rode madly on, as the animals responded to the lash.

Over hills and down through coulees the stampede led them. They reached the river, and though it was swollen it did not stop the men who had driven off the horses. In the darkness the pursuers could not distinguish the figures of the men, and it was useless to resort to weapons. They knew, too, that the horse-thieves would ride lying along the sides of the horses and thus escape being made a target for the pursuers' bullets.

In crossing the river, Bill and his party lost time, the stream being so swift that they were carried down for some distance before they could make a landing on the other side. The consequence was that the Indians who had driven off the horses were a long way ahead of their pursuers. It was evident that from their knowledge of the country the thieves were Indians and no strangers. The sound of their feet was still heard distinctly, and Bill urged his party to greater speed that they might yet overtake them.

The water was dripping from their clothes, but that was a slight matter if they could only succeed in gaining on the thieves.

Suddenly they found themselves in the midst of a band of horses scattered over the prairie, spent with the long chase, and wet with water and perspiration. No Indian was in sight. The horses were there, but where were the men who had driven them off? Had they been chasing a phantom? Had these horses been running of their own accord, or were they on the enchanted ground of the red man?

Fear took possession of the hearts of the bravest. Each man grasped his revolver and held his breath, expecting that an enemy would spring upon him from the darkness at any moment, or a well-armed band of warriors would pour a volley of shot into their ranks from some unseen vantage cover, or by stealthy craft seize them singly and destroy them.

A few moments passed, seeming like so many hours, when, reviving their courage, they rode among the spent horses and learned that they belonged to the white settlers, and had certainly been driven off by someone. Bill and his men held a short consultation. Darkness and Indians were the enemies of the white man, and until the day dawned they could not feel safe from danger. They scattered themselves among the horses and waited for daylight, listening for any sound that might give them warning of an approaching foe.

The early morning brought relief, and when exploring a narrow belt of brushwood one of the horses snorted and swerved aside from an old blanket that lay in a roll on the ground. They would have passed it by had not a groan from beneath attracted their attention. Turning, they saw the blanket move. Bill bent over it cautiously, and discovered an Indian in the last agony of death. Some of the men counselled shooting him to end his misery, but Bill knelt beside him and spoke a few words of peace. The man had been thrown from his horse as he stumbled, and had been so trampled on by the band of horses he had stolen that he had been able only to crawl into the bush and cover himself. Bill promised to tell his friends of his fate, and to let them bear away his body and lay it in the lodge of the dead. He knew the customs of the race, and how the women would mourn over the poor Indian's death: for, horse-thief as he was to the white man, he was a hero to his own people. The horses were returned to their respective owners, and one more story added to those told of Old Glad's son.

Chapter III.

The shadows of night had fallen about the lonely cabin as, with a tender light in his eyes, the old trapper continued in quiet, reminiscent strain:

"Yes, stranger, my Bill hev passed in his checks. I don't talk o' him often, fur it makes my heart sore to talk o' him. But ye seem interested, and it'll not do me any harm and mebbe do ye some good.

"My Bill wus allus tryin' to help somebody. There wusn't a man in all the country that could travel over the prairie like him. He knew every coulee. He wus a splendid guide and a good one. One day one o' his comrades started off fur the Missouri in the winter when the weather was fine. He wus ridin' and he didn't expect to be long on the road, so he didn't take much grub with him.

"He'd got away just two days when it come up a terrible snow-storm. I tell ye it wur enough to freeze the hair off yer head. The folks got anxious about him, but they wur all afeard to go out in the storm.

"Bill ses to them, 'I'm goin' to find him:' but they ses, 'It's no use, ye'll get lost yerself.'

"Wall, without tellin' anybody, he started off one morning, an' it wur cold; but he never heeded that.

He ses, 'I'm goin' to find him, dead or alive.' Ah, my Bill wus a brave fellow, an' as kind-hearted a fellow as ever lived.

"Two or three days went by, an' the storm kep' up, but Bill didn't turn up. The men in the Fort got anxious about him, an' so one night they talked together an' they agreed to wait another day, an' if he didn't turn up they'd send a party after him.

" It wur gettin' dark the next night when the men in the Fort see two ridin' on one horse, one in front o' the other, comin' over the prairie.

"They got out glasses an' made out that the one in front wus an Indian boy. He wus ridin' fast, an' the man behind him was muffled up an' had a cloth over his eyes.

"The men in the village went out to meet them, an' as they rode up they saw it wus Bill. He was snow-blind, an' his hands and feet wur frozen. He couldn't speak.

"The Indian boy told the men that as he wus comin' in from the Indian camp, he saw him ridin' slowly an' his reins wus thrown loose on his horse's neck, an' he wus trustin' to him to get to the Fort.

"The men in the Fort nursed him, but they thought he wouldn't get better.

" After lyin' still fur several hours, he ses, ' Is he gettin' better?'

"One o' the men sittin' beside his bed ses, 'Yes, ye're gettin' better.'

"Bill shook his head, but didn't say anythin'. After a while he cried out, 'I saved him. Is he gettin' better?'

"'Yes, yes, ye're gettin' better,' said another of the men.

"But a few minutes after Bill spoke again: 'The letter, the letter; read the letter!'

"'He is delerious, poor feller.'

"'Mebbe he had a letter from somebody,' spoke up one o' the men, an' they searched his pockets, an' sure 'nuff, found a small piece o' paper. It had some writin' on it with a pencil: something like this: 'Send some medicine as quick as ye can to save Jack's life. I left him at old Kootenay Brown's ranch. He was nearly frozen to death when I found him.'

"The men got an Indian boy, and sent him off with medicine an' a supply o' provisions to Kootenay Brown's.

"After Bill got a little better, he told the men where he had found Jack. He had an idea of the trail he would take, and after he'd crossed St. Mary's River, the storm was so bad that his horse wouldn't face it, so to save himself he struck toward the mountains. Wall, as he kep' travellin', the storm quieted down an', wud ye believe, right ahead o' him he saw a man walkin' round an' round in a circle leadin' his horse. The snow wur deep, but he went as fast as his horse would go, an' when he reached the place he saw it wus Jack.

"Both Jack an' the horse wur snow-blind, an' they wur wanderin' round on the prairie, lost. They couldn't get away from the spot.

"Bill's horse whinnied, an' the other stopped an' then answered. The poor thing wus glad o' company. Bill spoke to Jack, but the poor fellow didn't know him. He wus out o' his mind. Bill got him on his horse, and rode on to Kootenay Brown's ranch, where they rubbed poor Jack an' put him to bed. He wus badly frozen an' they feared he wouldn't get better.

"Bill stayed fur a day an' then started fur home to get help. It wus stormin' an' he thought he might get lef', so he wrote the letter afore he started out so that Jack might have his medicine.

"It wus a long time afore Jack wus well an' come back to the Fort, an' my Bill lay four weeks in his bed ; then he crawled round fur awhile, but he never got over his ride.

"Whenever anybody said anythin' to him, he would say, 'Never mind, it's all right : Jack got better.'

"All that winter an' the next summer he kep' about

SNOW-BLIND AND LOST ON THE PRAIRIE.

the Fort, coughin' bad. Ah, my heart wur sore to see him go like the snow on a summer day.

"Jack wud come over to his shanty an' do all his chores fur him, an' the two cronies would sit together fur hours.

"Jack wud look into Bill's face an' say, 'Bill, ye saved me, but lost yer own life,' an' then Bill, as best he could fur his cough, would say, 'Jack, it's all right: be a man an' help somebody else. One on us had to pass in his checks, an' it wus me this time. Yer turn will come too by an' by, mebbe afore ye think o' it. I've never done anything worth speakin' about. Ye know it's not because I wus unwillin', but, ye see, there's no chances o' doin' great things.'

"One day Jack an' Bill wur sittin' talkin', an' I went in ter see how he wus gettin' on, an' Jack wus talkin' like I never heard him afore. Ye'd a thought he wur a preacher. I think he must hev ben a good lad, fur I wusn't expectin' to hear the like.

" 'Bill,' ses he, 'I don't know much about the thing good folks call religion, but I min' my old mother tellin' me, "It's not long prayers an' talks, but it's just bein' like Himsel'." That wur what she called Him. I guess He'll no judge ye for the fine things ye say, but the gran' things ye do. He saw ye that day ye saved me when I wur frozen. An' don't ye think

He'll pay ye fur that? I'm sure He will. If I wur rich I'd give ye all I had, and they say He's honester than any o' us. An' that means if I canna pay ye, He will. Ye see ye must get yer pay fur doin' that gran' deed, an' I'm too poor to pay ye, so ye must look to Him for it.'

" ' I think it's all right, but it's not worth much,' says Bill.

" ' Worth much! It's worth all the world to me.'

" ' I wonder if He'll understand us when we get yonder. Ye see, we haven't been workin' much at religion, prayin', but, Jack, many's the time I have looked up at the stars an' said to myself, " Does God think about me!" Ye see the country is so big it wouldn't be strange if He forgot me.

" ' I've heard He lived on the prairie, and that makes me feel better, fur if He ever lived among the mountains an' on the prairies He'll know our rough ways an' not be hard on us. I don't think thur wus any fine churches an' fine clothes on the prairie when He wus livin'. If thur wus no prairie an' no mountains in heaven, an' all the folks talked fine language, I couldn't feel at home. I'd be like a stranger, an' I'd want to go where I could see the buffalo an' talk some Indian once in a while.'

" ' He wus a good man,' ses Jack, ' an' He wouldn't

be unreasonable, an' if we didn't talk fine here He wouldn't expec' us to talk fine yonder. I don't understan' much about it, but mother told me He wus a gentleman: not a rich, proud fellow who'd pass ye by, but a man who treated all alike. He could tell a rogue in fine clothes an' a gentleman if he wus poor.'

" ' I wonder, Jack, how I'll call on Him when I get yonder. Ye see, I've never been in company, an' I suppose a great many big folk will be crowdin' in the door, an' they'll be wantin' to keep me back. Will ye lift yer hat an' say, " Good day, sir," or will ye wait till He speaks to ye? I wish, Jack, ye'd go to the mission and ask the Sky Pilot that lives there: mebbe he can tell ye what to say. Mebbe he has books that'll tell ye, an' it's not the best thing to wait fur yer ticket till the last minute.'

" Before Bill could say any more Jack hobbled off, got on his horse, and rode fifteen miles to the mission house.

" The missionary wus at home, an' Jack wur surprised to see him wearin' a buckskin just like the trappers, an' he'd ben cuttin' out rails fur his fences an' had a axe in his hand. He greeted Jack civil, an' asked him what he could do for him. Jack just told him about my Bill, an' how he wanted to know what he wur to do.

15

" ' Can ye giv' a poor fellow directions what to do after he's passed in his checks, a kind o' passport like, to cheat the old fellow when he would be bettin' on the game.   Ye see, my pardner, Bill, that's nearly finished his game, an' you bet he's a good un, but he kind o' thinks he'd like to get posted afore he starts on the trip.   Ye can mebbe giv' us a prayer or a few words that we wouldn't be strangers.   We might fine it hard to get an interpreter.   Bill is pretty good at the Indian, an' he cud giv' them some Sioux or Cree, but the man at the door wouldn't understand. I'll pay ye for yer advice, fur he saved me, an' I hate to see him go: but I'll giv' him a good send-off an' a big funeral.'

"Stranger, the missionary came right off to my Bill, an' Jack, he wur proud to have the Sky Pilot ridin' beside him, an' when they come into the Fort the men looked at the stranger goin' to Bill's shanty, an' they ses, ' He's a rustler, that, an' don't ye forget it.   Ye bet yer life he'll see Bill through.   He'll treat him on the square ! '

" Bill's comrades wur sittin' round his bed talkin' when the prophet in buckskin, fur that wus what they called the missionary right there, come in.

" ' Good day, gentlemen,' ses he, an' takes off his hat, an' then sits down by Bill an' talks to him a bit to get a wee bit acquainted.   He ses :

" ' Wall, friend, what can I do fur you ? '

" ' D'ye think a chap'll lose the trail to heaven, that's never ridden over it afore ? '

" ' No, he'll get there all right if he follows the directions !' ses he.

" ' An' ye can giv' them to me, I reckon,' ses Bill.

" ' Yes: I haven't bin there, but the Chief has, an' He said afore He went off on His last trip that He would mark the trail so that His men wouldn't get lost.'

" ' Ye can tell me the marks He left. Is it a heap o' stones, or a tree blazed, or a fire burnin', so as I can see the smoke ? '

" ' I don't know what the marks are,' says the Sky Pilot; ' but, ye see, His ways are square, an' I know what He says is true. There's none o' the scouts ever come back to tell us. We are all tender-feet on that trail.'

" ' D'ye think they could o' lost it an' got down to the camp o' the old fellow ? '

" ' No: but when an old-timer starts on that trail he must like the place that he doesn't come back, or mebbe there's someone keepin' him there.'

" ' I guess he's struck it rich, an' he'll not come back,' says Bill, ' but how am I to know when I don't know the marks ? '

"'Wall, the Chief said afore He left on that long ride o' His that He'd make the way plain so that ye couldn't mistake it. an' He never wus false. All ye hev' to do is to pledge yerself afore ye start to join His ranks, an' He'll be there to meet ye, an' He'll take care o' ye Himself an' there'll be no mistake.'

"'Are ye sure that's so?' says Bill.

"'I'm sure. I hev served the Chief for many a year, an' I tell ye He wus never false.'

"Bill turned on his bed, an' as he looked at his old comrades, he says, 'Boys, I'm goin' on the long trail. Many a time hev we ridden on the prairie, but I'm goin' alone this time.'

"The Sky Pilot went down on his knees an' he prayed. It wus a right touchin' prayer, an' the men couldn't help the tears comin' in their eyes. Jack looked at Bill, an' says he, 'Bill's sure to pull through. If anybody can find the long trail, it's Bill.'

"It wus only a little while after that, stranger, that my Bill called out, 'He's waitin' fur me! Yes, I'm comin'!' an' his head fell back. My Bill was gone. Stranger, he wus a fine man."

The old man ceased. He had told the sorrow of his life. The stranger who listened knew no word was needed to express his sympathy, so with only a kindly grasp of the old trapper's hand he turned to the couch spread for him, and before many minutes had passed the occupants of the cabin were in a sound sleep.

The shanty among the hills still stands, and is yet the home of the grey-haired old-timer. As he sits at his doorway in the evening watching the shadows lengthen into night, memory often carries him back to the days when "my Bill" was the pride of his heart.

THE SPIRIT GUIDE.

THERE was a gay company assembled in the lodge of Eagle Rib, engaged in the pleasant pastime of tea-drinking and story-telling. The old chief had been successful in his late hunting expeditions, and from his sale of robes to the Indian traders a good supply of provisions had been brought to his lodge. A special invitation had been given to the leading members of the camp to attend the feast, and a large number had assembled to partake of the bounty in store. Every available pot and pan had been brought into requisition, and around the blazing lodge fire there stood vessels filled with buffalo meat, berries cooked in fat, and tea. The invited guests did full justice to the delicacies, both eating and drinking heartily. The pipe of peace was then passed around, and comments were freely made upon the conduct of those present who had been unfortunate in their hunting adventures. The stolid countenances of the Indians relaxed, and seriousness at times gave place to laughter loud and prolonged,

as one after another related some story of hunting,
love or war. The old men fought anew their battles
of former years, and as the feast proceeded, a spirit
of enthusiasm was begotten which infused itself into
the heart of every individual present.

An interested listener half reclined with his head
and shoulders on a native reed pillow; but his face
bore a stern expression, showing no sign of partici-
pation in the others' merriment, as if the perils and
victories of his fellows were nothing to him. Although
apparently heedless of his surroundings, yet he was
none the less a partaker of their pleasure. This
taciturn individual was Medicine Runner, a famous
chief of the Blackfoot Indians. Tall, stern and
dignified, he commanded the respect of all, and was
honored with the position of war chief of the tribe.
Though his hair was turning grey, there were no
signs of mental or physical decay. When he addressed
his people on any subject every tongue was silent,
all ears were opened to catch the words of the illus-
trious chief. He was a true orator, sparing in words,
but every sentence was full of meaning; and though
his language was couched in nature's garb, not even
the Indian trader could mistake its full import.
Many times he had led his warriors to victory when
contending with Cree, Crow or Sioux Indians. They

loved and honored him, while his enemies hated the name he bore. He lay for some time thus, a silent spectator of the joys of his companions. Then his eyes brightened, and he raised himself from his reclining position as if about to speak. The host and his guests knew at once the meaning of the change, and waited in respectful silence, anxious to hear what the chief had to say.

"Twenty-five winters have passed away," said he, "since a party of Sioux warriors entered our camp and stole a large number of horses. I was young and active then, and without any loss of time I called my warriors together that we might consult as to what was best to be done. After much deliberation at last I told them that I had prayed about the matter and felt it to be my duty to follow our enemies, taking another chief with me, while the warriors who remained in the camp were to be prepared for any sudden attack from the tribes who might be in our vicinity. I chose Three Bulls, who was at that time called Medicine Runner, to go with me on the expedition. We went out to the rock on the hill and made sacrifices and prayers. I prayed to my god for guidance, protection, and victory, and as I lay in my lodge at night, the god came to me in a vision, and told me to go, assuring me of an answer to my prayers.

We had a war dance and feast, painted our bodies and our horses with war paint, and then set out on our journey south. We had gone but a little way when I got off my horse and prayed again. I vowed that if successful and I was permitted to return I should sacrifice myself at the next sun dance.

"Four days we rode and saw not any signs of our foes, but as evening drew near on the fifth day we were pacing slowly on the plains when we came to the brow of a hill, and there right at our feet was a camp of Sioux Indians, numbering three hundred lodges. Our hearts beat fast when we saw so many lodges congregated together, and my companion expressed his determination to return that night, as it was impossible to do anything against such a strong foe. I remembered my prayers and my vow, and resolved to remain, though at the same time urging my companion to go home and to take my horse with him. He begged me not to throw away my life, but to accompany him and to bring back with us a large number of our warriors to help in slaying all the Sioux Indians. I told him I dare not consent, as my guardian spirit was driving me onward and I felt sure of victory, though alone.

"Three Bulls bade me a sad farewell, and taking my horse with him he rode away quickly in the direction of our camp.

"Again I prayed and resolved upon action. It was a dark night, and thus highly favored I waited until the middle of the night, that all the people might be asleep, watching meanwhile as closely as I could and studying the lodges in the camp. The time had come. I descended and entered the camp stealthily and unseen. Outside of a chief's lodge there was fastened a fine horse, a good buffalo runner, and this lodge I resolved to enter, examining my gun and knife to see that they were all right. I then peered into the lodge and saw the chief and his family quietly sleeping. Drawing the door gently back I went inside. A few dying embers lay upon the fire, and beside it stood a pot of meat. Feeling hungry I soon disposed of some of the food. I then took off one of my moccasins and left it that they might know an enemy had been there. Leaving the lodge as quietly as I entered, it was only the work of a minute to cut the horse loose, jump on his back and depart. Conscious of having gained the victory, and feeling safe on the back of such a fine animal, I could not refrain from uttering the war-whoop as I was leaving the camp. The greatest excitement prevailed when they heard it, and I knew that I would soon be pursued. They had heard the sound of the horse's hoofs, for presently several Sioux were on my track, yelling and beating

" As they approached I levelled my gun and shot the leader."

their horses to increase their speed. I had nothing to
fear, for a good horse and a good start were in my
favor. Most of my pursuers gave up the chase, and
finally I could hear distinctly the sounds of the hoofs
of but two horses following. Right ahead in the
darkness I could hear the sound of rushing waters. I
hastened on. Plunging into the foaming waters I
crossed the stream safely and turned suddenly around
as I reached the bank. Springing from my horse I
waited for my pursuers, and as they approached
levelled my gun and shot the leader. Before the
other could escape by advance or retreat I brought
him to the ground with another bullet. Victory
was assuredly mine, for now two scalps were fastened
to my belt, and I rejoiced that full compensation had
been made for the depredations of our enemies.

"Homeward I sped, resting occasionally to give
my horse time to recover his breath and refresh himself a little. When I reached our camp I heard the
women wailing for me as one dead, for they had given
up all hopes of my safety, but when the people saw
my approach and the scalps by my side their sorrow
was changed to songs of rejoicing. A great feast and
scalp dance were held. Three Bulls made a long
speech exalting my heroism, and ended by giving me
his name of Medicine Runner, which he then bore,
and which I have since borne until this day."

The chief had scarcely finished his story when a young man entered named Running Wolf. He was tall, slim, and of noble aspect, showing his relationship to the bravest of the tribe. He had a careworn appearance and was evidently suffering keenly from physical exhaustion : still a faint smile played upon his features and his eyes glistened with unusual brightness. Five days previous, this young man had gone from his lodge on an errand of some importance, as was evident by the determination which was expressed in the firmly compressed lips and the look of daring in his eye. For some time he had been very serious, and it had been remarked by some of the aged people that he seemed to be holding communion with the spirits. He withdrew within himself, saying little but thinking much, and the young man who formerly had been so full of merriment and delighted in all the amusements of the camp, had become suddenly transformed into a sedate man, almost prophetic in his looks. Without informing anyone of his intentions he had departed from his lodge, going rapidly toward the hills, apparently hoping to meet someone or determined to do some work. He walked quickly, shunning the presence of his companions, heeding not the riders who were driving herds of horses, and caring not for the scenes which always delighted him.

Old and young who saw him travelling at such a rapid pace across the prairie kept out of his way, for it was evident to their eyes that a supernatural power was guiding him. For many hours he travelled without halting, his eyes fastened on the ground, but with a holy purpose in his heart. Into one of the deep ravines he entered, and far into its recesses he travelled, where seldom penetrated the eyes of man, haunted as the Indians believed it to be by spirits of the dead, who possessed the power of inflicting injury upon the living.

It was in this community of spirits that Running Wolf found the resort which his soul longed for, its gloomy shades, rugged, tall rocks and scanty vegetation agreeing with the state of his soul. It was the home of the buzzard, coyote and eagle. Loveliness there was none, and as a resting place for man, no spot on earth could have been found more uninviting. This was the place, however, which seemed pleasing to the spirit of the young man, and for a few moments, although exhausted and sad, a gleam of satisfaction shone from his countenance. He fell upon his face kissing the ground, and in accents of tenderness cried, "My mother!" He lay upon the sod for a long time, fatigued with his journey and the physical exhaustion arising from nervous excitement, but at length arose, gathered his blanket upon his left arm, and began pacing to and fro, praying earnestly to the Great Sun for the revelation of himself.

Alone upon the hills and in the deep recesses of the ravines he wandered, praying and fasting, allowing nothing to pass his lips but a little water. Earnest, solemn and prolonged was his communion with the Great Power which overshadowed him, and the more keenly he felt this invisible presence the more fervently he prayed and longed for the fulfilment of his vows. Bright were his hopes, for he had implicit faith in the spiritual influences with which he was surrounded.

For days and nights the young man wandered alone, his voice heard by none save the spirits, the birds and the animals. At last he fell to the ground worn out with his devotions, and as he lay in a half-conscious state pleasant dreams flitted through his brain. The air was filled with happy voices. Angel attendants came to minister to him. Earth was no longer a weary place to live in, but the songs of joyous hearts came to him in all their sweetness, more pleasing than he had ever heard, and as he sang in unison with them, his heart was filled with joy. How long this continued he never knew, but in the midst of it all there came a voice assuring him of peace, the acceptance of his vows and prayers, and the gift of a Guide and spiritual Friend. The blessed vision rested on his soul as a rich benediction: and in this pleasant frame of mind he awoke. As he raised himself there came running toward him a small ground squirrel. This he seized instantly, and as he held the timid animal in his hand he remembered that this was the visitor named in his vision which would come to him, and within whose body would dwell the Spirit which was given him as a guide through life. As he held it, gently he drew it toward his bosom, and there nestling with fear it suddenly ceased breathing. His visitor was dead!

His heart was moved with sorrow; but he learned by the keen spiritual perception which had been given him that the Spirit Guide needed not a living agent wherein to dwell, for He could give animation if that were required.

Quietly and with reverence he laid the little thing upon the ground; tears filled his eyes. He prayed anew for guidance and strength, and as he prayed he took his knife and removed the skin of his little visitor and reverently preserved it.

A gentle voice whispered to him that the vision was ended. So casting a few quick glances around, he turned homeward, tired and footsore, but very happy.

A long journey lay before him. and in his fainting condition he could walk but feebly, yet so strong was his spirit that it overcame his physical weakness and enabled him to speed across the plains. New life had been granted him, and a companion of the spirits was now beside him wherever he went. As he drew near to the camp the dwellers fled at his approach. They beheld something supernatural in his manner which made them afraid. He entered the lodge of Eagle Rib as Medicine Runner finished his story, and without speaking a word sought his accustomed couch.

One by one the visitors left, impressed with the fact that some prophetic power had fallen upon the young man, and they dreaded contact with spiritual visitants.

These people are often called savages by members of the white race, yet they have been taught the greatest respect for all forms of religion, recognizing these forms as methods by which men approach the Supreme Power, hence their reverential attitude when the young man came into the lodge. In a few moments all the visitors had gone, and there remained only Eagle Rib and his family alone with Running Wolf.

He slept many hours, and then awaking fully refreshed, he partook of food, but said little to anyone. Becoming much reserved, not because of his superior position or knowledge, but rather because of the consciousness of this invisible companion, Running Wolf increased in favor with all the people. Gentle, sober and true, he won the hearts of the young men and maidens, who of all the natives of the lodges were most exacting.

A few uneventful years passed by, and the young man stood at the head of the young warriors of the camp, a recognized leader, well qualified to direct and destined to become victorious over every foe., His words were few, but when he spoke his judgment seldom erred, and his decision always carried away all opposition. Clothed with power and wisdom he had nothing to fear from any antagonist, and still he seemed unhappy. A restlessness of spirit appeared suddenly to take possession of him, compelling him to depart from the peace and happiness of the camp.

One evening, while sitting in the lodge, surrounded by his friends, without any word of warning or expression of any kind, he arose and departed, no one daring to follow, and no one asking the cause of his action.

The sun sank behind the Rocky Mountains, and

16

the prairie was soon enveloped in darkness, but the young man heeded not the deepening shadow; he was not afraid. He wandered far from the camp and entered the forest unnoticed and unpursued. Straight as an arrow he went onward until he came to the foot of a giant tree, and kneeling upon his knees, he breathed out a prayer, simple, majestic and brief.

Drawing his knife from its sheath, he began to dig vigorously under the sod, never resting in his eager search for some hidden prize. Presently from the depths of the soil he brought forth a tender rootlet, upon which he gazed with admiration, hugging it closely to his bosom as a treasure of rare value.

Then, quietly retracing his steps, he soon found rest in the lodge. No questions were asked, and few indeed were the words spoken, his reticent manner preventing any undue familiarity.

A few nights passed by and a messenger came to the lodge in deep sorrow, to inform Running Wolf that the daughter of Mastwena was very sick. Without manifesting any surprise, Running Wolf arose, went direct to the lodge of his friend where the sick child lay, and bending gently over her, he looked into the face of the little one. A gleam of satisfaction passed over his countenance. She was very sick, but not beyond hope of recovery.

The medicine drums were brought down and beaten to call to his aid the spirits which flitted from tree to tree and from stone to stone outside the lodge. The medicine song was chanted by all the members of the family, and Running Wolf sang vigorously as he swayed his body to and fro in an excited manner.

As he sang and prayed he drew from his medicine bag a piece of root, which he broke, and placing it in a vessel with a small quantity of oil, stirred it well. As he muttered words of import which acted as a charm to aid the medicine in performing its desired end, he gave it to the feverish child with the gentleness of a woman.

As the little one drank the medicine, he again repeated the strange words which had fallen from his lips, and although misunderstood by the members of the family, a shudder ran through the company, for they felt the sacred power which accompanied the casting out of the evil spirit which had taken possession of the child.

The child lay motionless for a few moments as Running Wolf prayed over her, and then a sudden change took place, the whole physical frame being strangely contorted through pain, the agony being almost unbearable. Heavy drops of sweat stood upon the child's forehead and rolled off her body, until as the

agony increased and the culminating point seemed to
be reached, she uttered a piercing cry, and then fell
back motionless upon her earthen couch.

Deep slumber fell upon her, and she lay asleep for
hours as if under the influence of a gentle opiate, no
one daring to arouse her, or caring to intrude upon
the territory of the home of the spirits.

As the sun arose in his splendor behind the hills
which lay across the prairie, the Indian maiden opened
her eyes, refreshed with her slumbers, free from pain
and the disease overcome. In a few days she was
running with her companions as strong and merry as
she had ever been.

The fame of Running Wolf was spreading fast and
was not confined to his own tribe, and had he been a
man of ordinary ability he would no doubt have
become elated over his success. Keeping his own
counsel he still felt humble, for he depended solely for
his success on the ministrations of the Spirit Guide
and the wondrous revelations which were frequently
made to him.

Many uneventful days were passed in the camp,
the severe illness of a friend or a skirmish with some
neighboring tribe alone breaking the monotony.

No counsel was more eagerly sought in the gatherings of the chiefs, and there was no chief in greater

demand as arbitrator in difficulties than Running Wolf.

He was loved for his wisdom, kindness and unassuming manner. The children listened to his stories as he sat in his lodge surrounded by the youth of the camp, who became so docile under his influence that with a single wave of his hand they quietly departed. Frequently they gathered around his lodge fire, and when the shadows of evening fell, they ran homeward to repeat the wonderful stories he had told them. Many a needless war was averted by his cool judgment and courage.

Late in the fall of the year this wise counsellor stood at his lodge door, and called aloud for his friends to attend a feast which he had made. A large company assembled to do honor to their friend. As they sat around in his spacious lodge, entertained by the conversation of the most notable men of the tribe, the evening passed away pleasantly. Running Wolf led off in the conversation late in the evening, and as he spoke in a tone of gravity, yet with a spirit of deep feeling, every ear listened and every heart beat in sympathy with the sentiments expressed. The orator proceeded to relate the history of the tribe, the story of its conquests, the records of the noble deeds of its great men, the advent of the white race and the present condition of the Indians. He depicted the future in dark colors, the gradual decay of the red men, the diseases and debauchery of the people, the corruption of the Indian politicians and the utter overthrow of the native religion. He counselled them to accept of the glory of the coming day when the red men would mingle with the white race, accepting their teachings and civilizations and finding therein peace, plenty and contentment. His voice faltered, and their hearts grew sad as he told them he would always remain with them to cheer them with his presence and encourage them by putting wise thoughts into their hearts; and he would touch the hearts of the white men, so that more tenderly than ever would they treat their brothers in red.

With downcast countenances they left his lodge and sought repose, although few of them slept because of the strange visions of the future his words had awakened in their minds.

Upon the following day a strange rumor spread rapidly over the camp that Running Wolf had not been seen after his great feast with the chiefs. Forebodings of dark destiny filled the minds of the people, and sorrow was depicted on every countenance. Women and children wept, and the men groaned in spirit, heavy with foreboding fears.

Running Wolf's favorite horse stood at the lodge door, his gun and military habiliments lay in their accustomed place, but the wise man was gone. A few footprints were seen leading out towards the prairie in the direction of the mountains, but after following them a short distance all traces of them were lost. Far and near they sought him but found him not.

Then the chiefs recalled the sadness of their hearts when he assured them he would always abide with them, encouraging their hearts and subduing their enemies. They now believe that he is true to his predictions, and that he still presides over them in a higher degree as chief among the spirits. Yet they cannot help going out every day to look across the prairie for the return of Running Wolf.

Some day he may return, but not as we look for him. As the guardian spirit of the tribe he still maintains his ascendancy over the people, and with greater power than ever he waits upon them in their counsels and religious feasts, no longer guided by the spirits, but himself a seer among the gods.

ALAHCASLA.

NAMUKTA, the aged chief, was dying. As he lay on his earthen bed in the buffalo-skin lodge, friends gathered in and now sat near, talking in low tones. While the old man's faltering voice rose and anon fell, in the delirious utterances of a fevered brain, they recounted his deeds of bravery and recalled his wise counsels.

Namukta was a great chief, a warrior who could tell more thrilling tales of encounters with the enemies of his tribe than any other among the lodges, and the young men had listened and had caught from his oft-repeated words the spirit of the warrior before they went upon the war-path. He was telling now of by-gone battles in the south, of victories won and scalp-locks taken from the foe; but his mind wandered and there was no connection in the talk.

Presently he ceased, and every eye was turned toward his couch. He was still for a few moments, and the people waited. Then the dying chief raised himself on his bed and called in clear, peremptory tones, " Isota ! Isota ! Isota !"

A young girl, fairer than any of the other maidens in the camp, yet dressed as one of them, rose from the buffalo-skin where she had been reclining, and crept nearer to the old chief's side.

"I am here, my father." But the chief made no reply. His ears were closed to the voice he loved, and the girl sighed as she resumed her seat.

Again he raised his voice and called aloud, "Isota! Isota! There they come! Lie still!"

He was fighting over again one of the battles of the past. In broken, disjointed sentences, bit by bit, Isota and the friends who were with him in the lodge heard the story told, which, put together, was something as follows:

"That was a hard time. It was the year of the rabbits. We had gone away to the east to hunt the deer, and we intended to take some horses from the Chippewas. Our young men had told us the Chippewas had some fine horses that they had taken from the white men. It was a long journey, but it was fine weather, and we had plenty of feed for our horses. When we reached the forests we saw tracks of the Chippewas. We kept a sharp lookout for our enemy.

"Early one morning we saw smoke from their camp-fires. We made ready to attack them: we would rush upon them unawares and defeat them. We sent out two of our young men, who brought back word that there were fifty lodges and the men were well armed. We consulted together, for it was no easy task to fight with so many, but we were ready and in good trim for fighting. We sent our young men again at night, and when they got back they reported that there were some fine horses in the camp, but some of the men were out hunting. We made up our minds to attack the camp early the next morning.

"There was not much sleep for us that night: we were too near the camp of our enemy. There were only twenty-five of our warriors, but they were all good men who had won many battles.

"Long before the sun was up we started for the camp, travelling quietly, and when we reached the camp we made a dash for the horses and fired into some of the lodges. The enemy rushed out, the men fighting and the women and children screaming. Five of the Blackfeet were killed, but we had ten scalps and thirty horses. As we were leaving the camp I saw a little pale-face sitting at the door of one of the lodges crying. I rushed to her quickly, picked her up and placed her on my saddle. The Chippewas were beaten and we did not care to fight any more. We had taken the scalps and the horses

and the little pale-face. That was a great fight. I
had the best part of it. You know my little pale-
face : I called her Isota."

Isota listened, her head resting on her hand. She
remembered being in the camp of another tribe of
Indians, but who they were or where they came from
or dwelt she knew not.

Namukta had ever treated the pale-face as a
princess, a child of the gods, for had not the gods
blessed his people ever since she had been in his
lodge? The men had not gone so frequently upon
the war-path, there was not so much sickness or
quarrelling in the camps. The maidens loved her
because she was ever ready to help them : she had
the finest skins for her dresses, and bear's claws and
elk teeth were used in plenty to decorate the lovely
Isota.

The chiefs consulted her on matters affecting their
bands of people, and wondered at her wisdom. Her
gentle manner, her calm dignity and queenly carriage
impressed them with a sense of superiority. They
believed she was possessed of many secrets not known
by the medicine-men, and this added to her influence
over the tribe.

Namukta guarded his treasure carefully, and there
was nothing too valuable to be given to his Indian

princess. And now Isota had tended him in his
sickness, and even the eldest of his wives had not
objected to this usurpation of her rights.

There was one other who loved the maiden as
fondly as Namukta. Alahcasla had been taken by the
Blackfeet during one of their raids upon some of the
numerous tribes of British Columbia, and because
Namukta was the war chief he had dwelt in his
lodge. Alahcasla was tall and handsome, and of an
intelligent countenance. He had played with Isota,
grown up with her, and loved her better than all the
world beside. Once when Isota had been attacked
by a bear, his trusty rifle had pierced the brain of
the savage animal and saved the girl's life.

Namukta, after the relation of the story of his
capture of Isota, lay for several days unconscious, but
when he drew near the border of the spirit-land
he awoke, conscious though very weak. He sum-
moned all the minor chiefs to his lodge, and divided
his property among his friends. His favorite horse
was given to Isota, and the next in value to Alahcasla.
Then turning to the peace chief he said:

"And now I am going to the sand hills and I leave
Isota and Alahcasla to protect the interests of our

"His trusty rifle had pierced the brain of the savage animal."

people. They cannot be chiefs, but they are greater than all the chiefs and medicine-men. If you consult them and follow their counsels you will never be led astray. Give them one of the best lodges, let them have a portion of all the game you kill, never go to war without seeking their advice, and you will become prosperous and happy. Good-bye, I am going. Bury me as an Indian warrior. I have done."

Namukta died and was buried with all the rites of his people, who mourned for him many days. His last instructions were obeyed, and while they followed the counsels of Alahcasla and Isota the tribe was prosperous.

Twelve months passed and some of the women saw that Isota's cheeks had lost their color; they talked of it among themselves, but said no word to Isota. Then one morning when the chiefs went to the lodge of their leader they found the widows and children of the camp weeping. Alahcasla and Isota were no longer in the lodge. No one had seen them since the night before, and the fear in their hearts was that their enemies had stolen Isota, and because of his love for her Alahcasla had followed. The tribe had heard of rumors among the Crow Indians and about the camp-fires of the Gros Ventres, that it would be a good thing if they could secure Isota, the white

leader, that prosperity might come to their lodges as
it had to Namukta, the old chief, and his people.

The chiefs held a consultation, and it was decided
that runners should be sent out to the territories of
the hostile Indians, and learn by stealth the fate of
their princess.

Far and wide they went, but could find no trace of
Isota. The people grieved, many of the children
sickened and died, the buffalo disappeared and the
warriors sat around in the lodges idle and dispirited.

Isota had departed and her people were to know
her no more.

.   .   .

"You bet yer life she's a beauty, an' don't ye
forget it. She's no Injun, that. She's got queer
tastes to be the wife o' an Injun, but he's a smart un,
none o' yer common prairie Injuns."

Such at all events was Dutch Fred's opinion. A
day or two before two travellers, an Indian and a
young woman of fair complexion, had arrived at
the ranch and been treated with more than the
usual hospitality by the head man. They had not
been very communicative, and after resting for two
days had ridden away north in the direction of the
line of white settlements. This and the superior
appearance of the pair had excited a good deal of

curiosity, and called forth the above expression of opinion.

Dutch Fred was right. Isota and Alahcasla were no common Indians. Namukta's story of how Isota had been brought to his lodge had sunk into the girl's heart, and as Alahcasla loved her better than himself, he was helping her to solve the mystery, although he knew that every day which brought her nearer to her own people took her farther from him and his love.

They had travelled many weary miles before they reached the Thunder Bay district. When Isota stood upon the shore of the great lake some memory was stirred within her, and a word long forgotten seemed to leap once more into life.

She knew that she had before stood beside a great sheet of water like this. Where was it? She could not tell. In vain she sought to recall something more definite than the vague sense of having seen broad sparkling waters such as this. She could not, but the train was set alight and here a word was to supply the needed clue—Huron !

They stayed that night with a band of Chippewa Indians who were camped on the shores, and as Isota lay in the wigwam weary and sad she heard the story of an old chief whom his people loved ; how he had grieved for and sought a pale-faced child that had been stolen. She had been entrusted to his keeping by the chief of another band, and while he was absent on a hunting expedition she had been carried away by a marauding band of Blackfeet.

Isota could not understand at first, but a long illness and the care bestowed upon her by the wife of the Chippewa chief gave her time to learn their language. It seemed to come back to her as a forgotten tongue.

When the sickness left her, Alahcasla, who had waited and watched beside her faithfully, brought the horses to the lodge door, and together they set out once more to reach the Huron country.

After many days of weary travel the shining waters of the lake lay before them. They had passed few settlements, but now the country was more cleared, and as the tall Indian and the beautiful Isota entered the long, straggling street of the pioneer towns they attracted considerable attention. Unused to the prying eyes and rude stare of ill-bred curiosity, Isota held herself more erect and Alahcasla drew closer to her side. During their stay in one of these frontier towns Isota's horse had sickened and died, and Alahcasla had put the girl upon his and walked by her side.

They were often faint for food and from weariness; they were not familiar with the ways of the white people, and did not know that they must ask for what they needed. It was not the Indian custom to ask for the hospitality that it was considered a privilege to be allowed to offer to the stranger within their lodges.

But the talk of the people in the streets had revived another link in the chain of Isota's memory of the past.

She heard the children call "Mother!" and immediately she knew the word had once been familiar to her lips. With these words "Huron" and "Mother" as talismans, the pair went on their way.

.   .   .   .

In one of the larger towns on the shore of Lake Huron, a crowd had gathered around two figures whose appearance was evidently causing considerable interest. Travel-stained, their once handsome dress of finely tanned and handsomely embroidered deerskin with beaded ornaments worn and discolored, Alahcasla stood, resentment in his eye and indignation expressed in every line of his tall, commanding figure, sternly eyeing the gaping crowd, while Isota leaned against the wall of the house, her whole attitude telling of weariness and despair. Her lips were

17

parched and dry, yet they still could utter the words,
" Huron," " Mother !"

Was there no one to respond : none to answer her ?

Presently a woman better dressed than the majority
among the crowd drew near, and with the kindliness
of a heart long softened by sorrow, and one which
found relief only in thought for others, she stayed to
ask the cause of the gathering there.

" Poor things," she said, as the crowd parted and
her eyes fell on the strange group; " they are surely
strangers here, and their proud bearing in such surroundings would lead one to suppose they are no
common people."

Isota looked into the kind grey eyes, and though
despair of ever being understood had filled her heart.
she uttered once again the words, " Huron," " Mother!"

A woman's sympathy and love for another had led
her to stay her steps and ask the cause of the gathering crowd, and now an answering echo in her heart,
a sorrow long borne, a wound made and never healed,
replied.   Isota and Alahcasla were taken home, the
one to her mother's arms, the other to seal with his
death the sacrifice of his love.

The long strain, the hardships of the journey from
which he had shielded Isota, and the confinement of
living in a house and amid crowded streets where his

free spirit could not breathe, was more than the child of the mountains and plain could bear.

Isota tended him faithfully and closed his eyes in death. Loving hands laid him to rest in the beautiful cemetery just outside the town. A simple stone was set up, bearing the names " Alahcasla and Isota," thus linking the living with the dead, and keeping alive the memory of the one who had sacrificed his own happiness that the woman he loved might be restored to her people.

THE HIDDEN TREASURE.

SNOW had fallen thick and fast during the night, and as we looked out over the prairie and saw it still being driven in long rolling drifts by the strong western wind, we shuddered and turned again gratefully to the fire within the house.

The cold was so intense on that winter morning that we were slow in getting out to our daily duties, a dilatoriness which we shared with our fellow-citizens of the frontier town. When late during the day we strolled down the street, we were struck by a change in the appearance of what had been one of the dreariest, most desolate and dilapidated houses in the place. The house had been vacant for some time, but there was on the morning of which we speak unmistakable evidence of life within its roughly built walls.

In the early spring three young men had paid our town a visit. They did not remain long; apparently they were not favorably impressed with its appearance or with the manner of its citizens. Our people were certainly not of a style to attract, nor did they on their part care for the presence of strangers. This peculiarity probably arose from the fact that respectable strangers seldom found their way there, and the townsmen had lost all desire to cultivate the acquaintance of any but those who belonged to the community. Being, as we have said, a frontier town, situated not far from the international boundary line, many fugitives from justice had sought refuge among us, and the presence of such an element was not conducive to the growth of the town, either socially or commercially. The shanties which these rough characters had made their homes were, during the long winter nights, veritable pandemoniums, and the looks and behavior of their occupants were sufficient to deter any honest young man from taking up residence among us. Many of the houses, like that we have described, had fallen into a dilapidated condition ; log buildings were falling to pieces, while in many of them factory cotton stretched over the sashes was the substitute for glass long since broken, or possibly never inserted. The roadways, too, were in a wretched condition, even on the one street the town could boast of.

It was little wonder, therefore, that the young men referred to had made so short a stay in the town.

Following the river, and choosing a beautiful site on
its banks farther north, they had pitched their buffalo-
skin lodge, and there they had lived for the months
preceding our story, cutting cord-wood, fishing and
shooting.

We had seen so little of these men that we did not
at first connect them with the altered appearance of
the old shanty on this bitter winter morning. In a
town like ours, the inhabitants of which were composed of such a heterogeneous mixture of men and
manners, we did not ask many questions of who or
what a man was, unless there appeared to be some
good cause for such inquiries. It was only after we
recognized in two of the young men the strangers
who had passed through the town in the early spring,
that the surmise occurred to us that the third might
be the inmate of the old house.

We learned that the poor fellow had been ill for
some time, and as he grew worse and the weather
more severe, his companions had decided to bring
him into the town, and see if any better help could
not be procured for him than they could give in their
camp.

The hearts of the rough and even the most wicked
men in the West beat tenderly for the helpless, and
it is well known that many of the most hardened

among them will give their last cent, aye, even their last crust, to aid such among them as are rendered helpless by accident, misfortune or disease. This characteristic trait of the old-timer was known to these strangers, and their confidence in the manifestation of sympathy for their friend was not misplaced. They had brought the sick man into town upon a rudely-made sled, taking the precaution to wrap him warmly in buffalo robe and blanket, that he might be protected from the cold. The journey over the smooth snow had been safely accomplished, but the bed they found in the rough shanty was of the barest description. They had, however, made the best they could of it. A curtain over the windows, the floor well swept, and the simple furniture, consisting of the merest necessaries, gave it at least a habitable appearance. Here his friends left him.

Learning the poor man was alone, we went to see him. At first, although it was evident he was anxious for sympathy and help, he regarded us with suspicion. The water left by his bedside was frozen in the cup, the fire had gone out, and the cold wind seemed to find its way through every crack and crevice in the rude log walls. The man was pale and emaciated, and, when spoken to, his replies were interrupted by the difficulty of breathing and pain of body.

"You have been sick for some time?" we asked.

"Yes—some—weeks."

"Where is your home?'

"In—Oregon."

"Are your parents living?"

"Yes."

"Have you any money?" A quick glance of suspicion was the only reply to this last question. We hastened to explain that we had no desire for his money, and our question was prompted only by a wish to help him.

"We have come to do what we can for you, and if you have no money, we can get some and use it for you, and see that you want for nothing."

"I guess—I'm not—down—to bed-rock—yet," was the muttered reply.

"Will you tell us your name?" we asked.

"Jerry—Lindley."

We needed no deep knowledge of the man to recognize that this was not his true name. We were not unprepared for it. Many of the old-timers had several, and it was not until we became intimate with them that we learned their true names.

We went again many times to see Jerry, and

always found him alone. It seemed strange that his companions should desert him, and we also noticed that the old-timers avoided his shanty. They were not as ready to afford him the aid usually given to the lonely and helpless, whose lot it was to be among them. Jerry was a castaway— ostracized by whiskey-traders and gamblers. Why or wherefore we failed to learn.

The weather grew colder, the sick man every day worse, and at last it became absolutely necessary to remove him to some warmer shelter than the old shanty. There was in the town an old man who was known by the name of Kamusi, a genuine speci- men of the "old-timer." He was rough and ready in language and manners, drank freely and gambled and grumbled continually, yet in all the country there was not a more tender-hearted man. He had an Indian wife and several half-breed children, whom he loved intensely and swore at incessantly. He led a careless, easy-going and, in some respects, a wild life, yet he was the most liberal giver to the Indian school and mission church. The log building, con- sisting of the kitchen, where Ling, the Chinaman, cooked, a small dining-room, a billiard and bar-room, which represented the hotel in the town, was owned and kept by Kamusi. This rough old man offered to take Jerry in and care for him free of expense.

We carried the sick man on a blanket, and laid him on an old mattress in the corner of the billiard-room. There, amid the strange surroundings of men and women, Indians, Mounted Police, half-breeds, traders, cowboys, and rough settlers, the sick man lay slowly dying. We went to see him frequently, and endeavored to lead his thoughts upward to higher things. The men at the billiard table, as we talked, would often lower their voices or play more quietly in deference to our presence, or it might be to the near approach of the deepening shadow of the death-angel's wings; and eager as they were over the games or the sums at stake, they gave many a thought to the dying man so near to them.

We had succeeded in getting a doctor to look at him, but he could do no more than repeat our own opinion that the man had not long to live. As we tried to tell him of the way of peace, and prayed, our hands resting on the side of the billiard table, the gamesters ceased, doffed their hats, and let their cues rest on the floor. Such a prayer-meeting, in such a place and with such a congregation, could not but leave abiding memories in many hearts, and, we trust, led some to better living.

A few days before his death one of Jerry's old comrades returned, and by his devoted attention and continuous watch over the dying man aroused the suspicions of some of the men who frequented the billiard-room. Rumors were soon floating about that Jerry was known to have possessed several hundred dollars. No one knew where it was hidden, and the general opinion was that Tom Hastings was after no good.

One night just before Jerry died, and after a draught had been given him to ease the pain he was suffering, he seemed anxious to communicate some intelligence. Unable to speak, he traced, with feeble, trembling fingers, some straggling characters on the wall against which he lay. We could not decipher their meaning, but the men standing near seemed to understand. Presently two of them mounted their horses and rode out of the town.

Jerry died the next day, and we buried him on the prairie. No one, not even his two "pals," knew or could tell where Jerry came from. We made some inquiries, but failed to find any of his relatives or obtain information of where his parents lived. We knew no more about him than what he had told us himself in answer to our first questions.

Some days after his companion's death, Tom Hastings went south with an ox-train. Before he left he paid all who had incurred any expense in befriending

the sick man. Pete Rowley, the third of the trio,
remained in the country and seemed to prosper for
a time. He never worked, but was always well
dressed and appeared to have all the money he
required. After hovering about the billiard tables
for several months he disappeared. No one cared
to ask where he had gone.

What the writing on the wall betrayed, who had
found the treasure whose hiding-place Jerry's trembling hand had described, we never knew; but we
often thought that if wrong had been done by any
or either of his friends, a day of retribution would
surely come to the one who had acquired it, and the
mystery surrounding it would then be fully revealed.

THE WHITE MAN'S BRIDE.

THE Blood Indian camp was pitched on one of the bottoms of the Kootenay River, and with its two hundred or more lodges formed a picturesque group, the painted buffalo-skins of the lodges and the gay attire of the numerous Indians who rode in and out among them and on the surrounding prairie, making a brilliant and attractive scene.

There was unusual excitement in the camp on the evening on which our story opens. This excitement was most noticeable among the female portion of it, and was caused by the arrival of Major Brown, an Englishman, and a fine specimen of that educated class of his countrymen who, being possessed of private means, are able to indulge their desire of change and adventure. White men had visited the camp before; some had even made their homes for a few months among the tribe, but never at any time had so much interest and curiosity been excited, or so many questioning glances been exchanged between the women as on the arrival of this particular Englishman.

Major Brown's personal appearance was doubtless a sufficient reason for the unwonted stir among the women, especially in the lodges where the younger ones dwelt. He certainly was a handsome man, and, in conscious indifference to its effect, bore himself in a dignified manner among the people. Belonging to an old family of noble lineage, his youth had been spent in one of the best public schools: two years of hard work at Oxford had followed, and the foundation of a good education laid. Unable, owing to a lack of fortune, to maintain the position his birth and education had entitled him to in the Old World, he determined at the close of the two years' residence in the University to seek a home where he might in a short time earn sufficient to enable him to start a good business in England, and eventually become one of her merchant princes. His friends tried to dissuade him from carrying out this plan, but without success. He had heard of the Indians, had read much of the sport to be had, of the freedom of the life in the north-western part of Canada, and the conditions of existence appeared so fascinating to him, so attractive in comparison with the formality and convention-

ality of social life at home, that he could not be
induced to give up a prospect of pleasant adventure
for the present and possible prosperity for the future
to live a narrow life hampered by want of means at
home. Therefore bidding his friends farewell, he set
out for the New World, resolved to make a stay of
some years in the far West. He arrived in the
country at the time when a great gathering of the
tribes—Crees, Stoneys, Blackfeet, Piegans, Bloods and
Sarcees—was assembled at the Blackfoot Crossing.

The tribes had been invited to meet the representatives of the Government at Blackfoot Crossing.
Having implicit confidence in the Great Mother, the
Queen, they made their way to the place of meeting. There were assembled nearly three thousand
belonging to the different tribes when Major Brown
arrived. He was much impressed with the people,
and listened in amazement to the oratory of Crowfoot, Red Crow and Bear's-paw, notable chiefs of the
Blackfoot, Blood and Cree tribes. The Government
Commissioners addressed the people in the name of
the Queen, urging them to make a treaty surrender-
ing their lands to her for the benefit of her subjects,
and assuring them that she would compensate them
amply for their loyalty.

It seemed a difficult matter for the Indians to

give up the lands whereon they had dwelt so long, and to allow the white man to come in and take possession, but they knew that every promise which had hitherto been made to them in the Queen's name had been faithfully fulfilled, and that the advice given them was for their good.

The great chief of the Blackfeet, Crowfoot, arose, and addressing the Commissioners in the presence of the large assemblage, said, in the impressive manner of which he was a master:

"While I speak, be kind and patient. I have to speak to my people, who are numerous, and who rely upon me to follow that course which in the future will tend to their good. The plains are large and wide. We are the children of the plains. It is our home, and the buffalo has always been our food. I hope you look upon the Bloods, Blackfeet and Sarcees as your children now, and that you will be indulgent and charitable to them. They all expect me to speak now for them, and I trust that the Great Spirit will put it into their breasts—into the minds of the men, women and children and their future generations— to be a good people.

"The advice given me and my people has proved to be very good. If the police had not come to this country, where would we all be now? Bad men and whiskey men were killing us so fast that very few, indeed, of us would have been left to-day. The police have protected us as the feathers of the bird protect it from the frosts of winter. I wish them good, and trust that all our hearts will increase in goodness from this time forward. I am satisfied: I will sign the treaty."

Several others spoke, but they for the most part repeated what Crowfoot had said. At last the terms of the treaty being fully explained and understood, the names of the chiefs were written in the native language, and the men signed it with their marks or totems.

Food was given the people, and the chiefs accepted the officers' uniforms and medals which were given in commemoration of the event. After being informed that they would receive their money payments regularly every year, the vast assembly dispersed.

Major Brown was busy among the people, and through the aid of one of the interpreters he made many friends among the red men.

A large detachment of Mounted Police travelled southward until they came to the prairie village on the banks of the Old Man's River, where they had erected their barracks of logs and mud. The Major accompanied them, and was not long in getting a

18

position as clerk in one of the trading establishments in the primitive-looking town, where by his manly bearing and genial disposition he very soon made friends among the white people and the red men.

After breaking up their camp the Indians started southward on a buffalo hunt, and few of them were again seen until about the time when they returned for the annual treaty payment. They met on the banks of the Kootenay River, pitched their camp and then rode into the prairie village to receive their annuities.

Several thousands of dollars were paid, for each received five dollars per annum—men, women and children—the chiefs receiving ten dollars and the head chief twenty-five dollars.

As soon as the payments were over Major Brown set out with three men and a large supply of goods for the Indian camp, and it was upon his arrival that the women were struck with the handsome appearance of the tall Englishman.

A large tent was pitched, and the people gathered in large numbers to feast their eyes, like little children, upon the great display. Blankets, beads, tea, tobacco, fancy pipes, shirts, belts, guns and various kinds of cloth in fancy colors attracted young and old.

The presence of the Mounted Police in the country had made it possible for this handful of men to expose their goods in this loose fashion among the people. In the days previous to the advent of this force of red-coats the trading was done in a very different fashion. Formerly the traders built a log fort, which they fortified with a high stockade. A few Indians were allowed to enter for the purpose of trading, and while they stood at the counter they were guarded by men who had rifles, ready to shoot them down if they showed any intention of stealing, or acted in a spirit of enmity. Brawls were frequent under such conditions, as some of the traders were unscrupulous, and when under the influence of liquor took advantage of the natives.

The Major had picked up some of the common words among the people, and was able to make himself understood. A brisk trade was done in the camp for several days. The Indians were paid in one-dollar bills, as they did not understand bills of a larger denomination.

Five women were seated in a lodge conversing while the men were visiting their friends or buying goods at the trading tent.

One of them spoke up saying, " Have you seen the tall man ? " and another said, " Yes; have you seen the white chief?" "He is a handsome man!" "He has a good temper!" "He does not get angry!" "He is always smiling!"

With expressions such as these, mingled with a gentle titter, the women talked about the man who was in charge of the tent.

"Has he a wife?"

"No! he has not any," replied one of the women. "I was at his lodge and I did not see any woman there, and he has not another tent in the camp."

"He is like all other white men: he does not care for an Indian woman," ejaculated another.

"No! he is not like others; he is a far better looking man, and he would not treat an Indian woman like them. He has too good a heart."

"I would not trust him. He is like all the others. They are all alike. My chief says they are all the same. They look very pleasant, but they have the heart of a snake."

In the lodge sat a young woman who took no part in the conversation, and yet listened intently to the words of the others. She was an interested listener, but with the quiet demeanor of an Indian her countenance was unmoved while they were speaking. She was a comely maiden of about fifteen or sixteen years, whom her father loved so much that he would not give her to any of the men in the camp; thus she had remained unmarried longer than was generally the case. She was modest and beautiful, dressed neatly and worked hard. She, too, had seen the white chief, as they called Major Brown, for she had accompanied her father several times to trade. He had even spoken to her, and she had replied in her own quiet way to his questions when her father signified his desire for her to speak. It was not, therefore, an uninteresting conversation to her, although she refrained from discussing his personal appearance or character.

"Come, Napiake, what do you think of the white chief?" asked one of the women.

"I don't think anything about him," she replied, in her modest way.

"Oh, yes, you do," replied one of the group. "You do not go to the trading tent with your father every day for nothing."

She was silent, however, upon this subject, and although the women tried to draw her out by their questions they failed. It could not be doubted, however, from the expression of her eye, that she had experienced some emotion when the subject was touched upon, but from her manner she seemed to care little about the matter. This may have arisen from her womanly nature. At any rate she remained quiet while the women talked on upon a topic so pleasing to them.

After the busy time was over, the white men determined to remain two or three days longer, and during this period Major Brown was a frequent visitor at the old man's lodge. He seldom came without bringing some tobacco or other present to the chief, and although he did not understand much of the native language, he listened respectfully while the chief would relate in his own animated style the thrilling tales of his early days.

The Major was able to follow him to some extent in his stories, and at any rate he seemed delighted with what the old man said, which pleased his host very much. Napiake sat in the lodge an interested listener.

The tent at last was cleared of all the goods and placed on the large wagon, and in a few hours they would take their departure for town. Major Brown bought a fine horse and made a present of it to the chief, with a gun and some provisions. He then turned to the young woman and simply said, "Napiake." The father nodded his head, spoke a few words to her in the Blackfoot tongue, and the girl arose, dressed herself and followed Major Brown.

The women peered from the doors of their lodges, but Napiake cared not, for well she knew that some of them would be jealous and others delighted that she was the wife of the white chief. Unceremonious it might seem to the civilized, but Napiake had long expected that some day she would have to go forth at the bidding of her father to be the wife of some Indian who would take her father's fancy, or reward him well, so that his love would be outweighed. The time had come, and she had got better than an Indian chief for her husband, and the maiden was delighted beyond measure. She had heard that the white men had only one wife each, and that they were kind to them, so felt that she was elevated above the Indian maidens in thus becoming the sole wife of one man. Unregretfully she left her father's lodge, for she was going not more than a day's journey distant, so that she could see her kin often; besides she had remained at home full two years longer than the maidens of her camp, and she felt grateful to her father for his love.

Major Brown was a happy man as this beautiful Indian woman of tender years followed him at a close distance. He was following the custom of the white men in the country in taking an Indian woman for his wife. He placed her upon the wagon and along with the men she went to town. She found a home

for two weeks with the Indian wife of one of the white
men in town, and during this time the Major built
a small log-house, neat and comfortable, and furnished
it well. Napiake was pleased to have a house of her
own, and she set to work to make it as attractive as
she could for her husband. As husband and wife
they were happy and contented. He had a good
situation, was steady and industrious, and she was
tidy, hard working, and faithful.

A babe was born to them and their cup of happiness seemed full. He was the welcome heir of the
log mansion, the father's pride and the mother's joy.
At night when the heavy day's work was done, the
Major would dandle the child on his knee, and sing
and coo to him. He was happy, and nothing could
induce him to leave his home in the evenings. The
babe resembled his father, a fact of which both
parents were proud.

The child was only a few months old when Major
Brown received instructions to proceed to Pincher
Creek, nearly forty miles distant, with a supply of
goods to trade with a camp of Indians located there.
The Major and Napiake went along with the other
members of the party who were to accompany them.

A few days were spent with the Indians near the
mountains, and upon their return home, the mail

having arrived, the Major found some important letters awaiting him from the home land. The business of the camp for a time kept him later than usual at his office, but after the busy season was over, he informed Napiake that he was going to give her a visit of a few days in the camp with her friends, and during her absence he would start off to the mountains on a hunting expedition.

Napiake was delighted with the idea, as she had seen the Major's face for the past few days was paler than usual, and felt sure that a hunting expedition to the mountains would restore the color to his cheeks. She began at once to make clothes for her babe, that she might show him off to advantage in the lodges of her people.

The day came for her departure, and the Major took her and the child to the lodges of her people. Napiake and her babe were received with great joy, and her husband welcomed, for the Major had not been in the camp more than twice since the day that he took Napiaka from her home. Nearly three years had passed since she departed with the Major, but it had been such a happy period that it seemed but as yesterday since she turned her back upon her father's home.

Major Brown returned to the camp at the time

promised for Napiake and his child, and the aged chief was delighted to see him. The Major took his wife and child to their home, and was as happy as ever in their company. Napiake said nothing to him about what she had heard in the camp, for she had trusted him, and he seemed to be worthy of all her confidence.

A few months passed by and another babe was born. The Indians came to see the fair skinned babe, whom they named Morning Star. She shed her light for a while in the home, and then it was suddenly extinguished. The child sickened and died, and great was the sorrow of the household at her loss. But there is always a blessing in affliction, uniting the hearts of the sorrowing ones more firmly together and increasing their love for each other. And it was so in this instance. The Major could not do enough for his wife to soothe her heart for the loss of the babe. Little Morning Star was placed in a beautiful coffin, and laid away to rest in the ground beside the graves of the white men in the settlement.

Napiake often wandered with her little boy to the grave of her darling, and sitting beside it she would pour out her grief. So intense was it that she oftentimes forgot to go home, and the Major would find her weeping by the spot. The father was sad, but

"Napiako," he said sadly, "I am going on a long journey across the sea."

he restrained his grief and endeavored to comfort his wife.

One evening after the mail had come in, Major Brown came home with a serious countenance. His wife and child met him at the door. At once his serious mood disappeared and he was himself again. He dandled his boy upon his knee and talked cheerfully to Napiake. Supper over, he drew a large envelope from his pocket, and opening the letter it contained, read it inaudibly, but with an earnest, serious expression on his face. His wife busied herself about her household duties, glancing occasionally at the Major as he sat poring over his letter.

"Napiake," he said sadly, "I am going on a long journey across the sea. I have some important business to attend to at my old home, and I must go there to look after it."

The woman stopped her work as the Major uttered these words, a great fear coming into her heart.

"May I not go with you and make you happy among your people? I am willing to go anywhere with you," she said, as she looked steadfastly in his face.

"That would never do, Napiake, to take you away from your own people."

The tears started to her eyes. Was her devoted

husband going to leave her, and would he never return? Perhaps he might follow the example of others, and leave her. No, that was impossible. He was too good. She never had cause to doubt his faithfulness, and she knew that he would either take her or return to dwell in the country.

"When are you coming back?" she asked timorously.

"I shall be absent about a year, and then I will return, and we shall never again be parted."

Napiake gazed earnestly at him through her falling tears, but his glance was so honest and true that she said, "Well!" Not a word more escaped her lips, but the tears ran freely down her cheeks.

In a few weeks the Major had all his matters arranged and was ready to leave. A few minor matters had to be attended to, so he took his wife and child to camp. The aged chief received him with marks of esteem. He loved his son-in-law, and thought there was no one in all the country equal to him for ability, and he never tired telling his friends that the Major was a handsome man.

The Major related his plans to his father-in-law, who listened attentively, and when he had finished he placed a sum of money in the hands of the old man.

Early next morning as he bade them farewell, a large party stood around the lodge to see him depart. He stooped and kissed Napiake and his son, and with a wave of his hand, drove away.

A grand banquet was given the Major in town by his friends, many of whom came miles to attend this farewell supper, for he was a great favorite with all. A large crowd gathered about the stage-coach to shake hands with him as he said good-bye to one and all.

That same evening there were a number of his friends in the neighboring town of Leighton to see him off at the little railroad station. The night was dark, and as he stood in the circle of friends, he excused himself for a moment and stepped aside. There in the gloom stood an Indian woman with her boy, looking on and weeping. It was Napiake and her child who had come a distance of thirty miles to get a last glimpse of him. Faithful to the last, there she stood, weeping disconsolately.

The Major was touched by this evidence of her devotion to him, but as he strove to comfort her the conductor shouted, "All aboard!" the engine whistled, and the Major, placing a sum of money in the hands of each, kissed them both, sprang upon the train, and was gone. Napiake and the boy watched the retreating train until it disappeared in the darkness, and then sadly retraced their way to the camp.

"I'll give you two horses for her," said Pinakwaiem.

"Two horses are not enough. She is a good worker, and she is young, and you know she can talk English, and is a good housekeeper, for she was the wife of the white chief."

"The wife of the white chief! And that's the reason she is not worth so much. I'll give you the two horses."

"All right, you can have her."

Napiake, after waiting patiently for two years for the return of her white chief, had become the wife of an old Indian, sold for two horses and destined to slavery. Pinakwaiem led Napiake and her son to his lodge. Not a word escaped from the patient woman. As a sheep led to the slaughter she was dumb, submissively following the man who had bought her, for she was now his wife according to the Indian custom. There were three women already in the lodge to which she was going who were recognized as wives, and Napiake as the latest addition held a good position for a while amongst them. The old man then treated them well, and she seemed to have a hold upon his affections. She did her work faithfully, uttering no word of complaint. But in a few months the novelty of the new life wore off, and Pinakwaiem began to treat her harshly. It was not hard for him to see that her heart was not with him. Napiake never smiled, and seldom spoke. Her life was sad and hard. She carried the wood from the bush on her back, the burden bending her almost in two, and bore large pails full of water a long distance from the stream. Her little boy seemed to be always in the way; he was scolded, but never struck, for the customs of the natives frown upon the harsh treatment of children.

The old life and the new were in strange contrast. She had become the drudge of the lodge and the most despised of the wives of the old man. Doomed as she now was to a life of sadness, toil and oppression, all hope died out of her heart and she had no delight in any of the amusements of the camp.

Sometimes the name of the white chief was mentioned in her presence as a taunt, and stung with the remembrance of her former treatment, Napiake sought peace in the solitude of the bush or by the river, where she sat for hours with her little boy by her side. She gave not railing for railing. The sweet and beautiful countenance of the former days had fled, and given place to a haggard expression which made

her appear to be an old woman, as she dragged her
wearied limbs through the camp. Some of the Indians
jeered at her, but others pitied her in her loneliness
and grief. The thought of her boy alone sustained
her, and by a great effort she determined to live for
him.

She could not flee to another camp, there was no
place for her among the white people, divorce there
was none, and she hoped that some day her Indian
husband might sell her to another Indian who might
treat her more humanely. But the seeds of disease
were sown in her system, and she was already doomed
to fall a victim to the curse of the Indians, that fell
destroyer, consumption.

The medicine drum was beaten night after night,
and the song and prayers of the medicine-man sounded
through the camp. But all was of no avail; Napiake's
life was slowly ebbing away.

Late one night there entered the lodge a white man,
dignified and grave. The Indians gave him the seat
of honor in the lodge. He knelt beside the sick
woman, beautiful now as ever in the days of health.
The haggard looks had disappeared, and a peaceful
contentment rested upon her face. The visitor spoke
in a low tone, and Napiake listened, attentively
answering his questions. Her father and friends

leaned forward to catch her faintly expressed words. After some quiet conversation, raising herself in a state of excitement and looking the missionary in the face, Napiake inquired:

"Shall we see each other there?"

"Yes, in the land of God, we shall see each other."

"Shall we know each other?" eagerly asked the woman upon whose countenance the shadow of the death-angel had fallen.

"Yes," was the simple answer of the man.

"I shall see him! I shall see him! Shall we live there always?"

"Yes, we shall, never to be parted again!"

Napiake fell back upon her couch, saying, "I'm satisfied, I'm satisfied! God is just."

A few heavings of the breast and the hands fell by her side. Napiake, the beautiful Blackfoot woman, was at rest.

In a large and busy manufacturing town in the west of England, a merchant sat in his office reading his letters. At the door stood a coach with a pair of handsome horses: seated in it a lady with a babe upon her knee.

"Tell your master that I am waiting," said she to the footman, who promptly obeyed the command.

19

" I will be there in a few minutes," was the reply. The merchant seldom went for a drive, his extensive business usually requiring his whole attention; but he had made up his mind to spend this afternoon with his wife and child. The letter-carrier had just delivered his mail, and he was hastening to give directions to the letter clerks to answer them before leaving.

Among the others was a paper from the Canadian North-West, in which a marked paragraph caught his eye:

"There died last Friday, on the Blood Reserve, Napiake, an Indian squaw. Some of the pioneers of the district may remember her as a beautiful woman when she was young, who lived for a time in the village in the early days."

Turning suddenly pale, he laid the paper aside and left the office. As he sat in the coach his wife pointed to several objects of interest which they passed, chatting freely about them, but he paid little attention. It was as though he heard her not. All her efforts to drive away his morose silence were in vain. Far away at the foot of the Rocky Mountains the husband saw a woman dying in an Indian lodge, a woman who loved him to the last, but whom he had deserted and forgotten. Forgotten? No! He could never forget her.

But in that busy English town he is a merchant prince, holding an honored position in society. He is a member of several societies, and is often speaking on behalf of the enfranchisement of women and popular education.

Sometimes an old man leading a boy by the hand may be seen standing beside a mound on the wide prairie of the West, but there is no other that ever visits that lonely grave.

Little Charlie Brown finds a home among the Indians, depending on them for food and clothing, and sometimes an old-timer takes compassion upon the boy and gives him a morsel of food or some clothing. He endures the poverty of an Indian lodge, while over the sea his father enjoys the comforts of an English mansion.

THE COMING OF APAUAKAS.

NIGHT after night during the long and dreary winter, from where the lodges were pitched among the small patches of timber that fringed the river bank, came the low, monotonous beating of the medicine-drums, a sad refrain telling the story of sickness and death.

"Take pity on me! Take pity on me!" floated upon the evening air, a wail from the lips of the aged warrior as he lay on his earthen couch and wrestled with the grim spirits who were waiting for his soul.

Thick clouds of pestilential fever hung over the camp. The ruddy glow of the lodge fires served but to deepen the gloom. The happy hunting days were gone; the excitement of the buffalo chase was a thing of the past. The ancient traditions of the coming of a race of white men who were superior in numbers and strength were now being fulfilled, and the hearts of the mourners in the camp by the river were heavy. "Take pity on me!" was the burden of their song. Strong men bowed their heads as they uttered the plaintive words; the women wept and prayed. The children alone were merry and wondered why their mothers were sad.

In the deep recesses of the wood, high in the forks of the trees, the dead lay still and cold, freed from the pain and poverty of the plague-stricken camps. No angel visitant came with mercy in her hands to relieve the sick or to bestow gifts upon the poor. Forsaken by friends and foes, the dying turned from their friends and sighed their lives away.

Night had closed in upon the desolate scene, and the dwellers in the lodges were seeking what rest they might, when a sharp cry rent the air causing many to raise their heads and listen. But it was no warning shout of danger; it was only the wail of a stricken heart. A father had returned from the mountains, whither he had gone in quest of game, and on entering his lodge found none to meet him save an aged medicine-woman. Wife, sister and children had all been called to the spirit-land. His hearth was desolate; the song and the prattle of merry childhood which had always greeted his home-coming were silenced forever. Throwing himself upon the ground he wailed forth his anguish in the cry that had startled the sleeping camp.

Hope had well-nigh died in the breasts of the

people. Their medicine-men's charms no longer protected them from sickness, and their guardian spirits
had abandoned them in the hour of distress. They
prayed and longed for release from the pain and
burden of life. Yet a few days more and their
prayers would be answered.

The morning sun was gilding the eastern horizon
as a young man, footsore and weary, drew near the
camp and ran eagerly toward the chief's lodge.

"What news? What news?" asked the people of
each other, but none could reply. The men dragged
themselves to the lodge where the young man waited
impatiently the coming of the chief. The latter
entered presently with his friends, and in obedience
to his command the young man delivered his message
before them all.

"Chief: It is now three moons since I left my
people here and travelled toward the northern land,
where dwell the Sarcees, Crees and Stoneys. I went
to a large camp of the Crees. The people received
me in kindness and supplied me with every need.
Their hearts were filled with joy and they sang from
daylight till the darkness fell. There was abundance
of food; the medicine-man's drum had ceased to beat,
there was no sickness in their camps. Guardian
spirits hovered over the lodges, and as I sat day after

day among the people I listened to songs and stories that were strange to my ears. I waited for the feasts that we ofttimes have in our own camps that I might take part in the amusements of my people, but as I spoke of these things they gazed at me in astonishment and pity. I became angry and would have departed had not an aged chief named Jacob come into the lodge.

" The old chief looked upon me with kindness in his eyes and addressed me in my native tongue. He related to me the tales of my childhood and my heart was glad. I had found a spirit kindred to my own. He spoke of the 'Old Man of the Mountains,' the 'Blood Clot Boy,' the 'Morning Star' and all the wonderful things they had done.

" ' Your fathers have told you, young man,' he said, ' of the coming of a tribe vast in numbers and different in color and habits from the Indians of the plains. You have listened in the lodges of the south to the story of the great hero Apauakas, who is to come bringing blessings in his hands for all the people. When he comes the buffalo shall increase in number, the people shall have food in plenty and shall not need to toil so hard. The land shall obey his command, the rivers shall have many fishes, the mountains and prairies be covered with antelope, sheep and goats.

The wolf and the bear shall flee away into the secret places of the hills, and no longer shall they molest us. Our camp shall be filled with children and happy mothers. My son, the Great Chief is coming! coming!'

"My heart was filled with joy as I listened to his words, and I longed for the coming of Apauakas. The chief had risen as he thus spoke kindly to me, but was silent. He struggled to control his emotions, then leaning forward and gazing earnestly into my face he said slowly:

"'Young man, the white tribe has come, the prophecy is fulfilled. All over the prairie the men and women of the white tribe are building their lodges. The buffalo have fled before their presence, disease and death have spread desolation among our camps. The land of our fathers has been taken from us, the Indian race is doomed to depart before the feet of the white stranger and we dwell in the land of an enemy. Would that I had died before I had seen this hour: I had then been spared the pain and anguish that have fallen upon us.'

"As he ceased, smitten with sorrow and anger, I laid my hand upon my knife, determined to depart and slay the oppressor or drive him from the land. But the chief spoke again.

"'I am not done,' he said. 'When I think of the

happy days enjoyed by my people I am silent, though the warm blood coursing through my veins makes it hard to restrain my anger. One day as we sat in our lodges nursing our sick in sadness, while the medicine-men beat their drums and prayed, there came to our camp from the lodges of the white tribe a pale-faced man. He could not speak our language, but he made signs that he wished to live with us. We suffered him to stay, and gave him a share of our scanty food.

"'Every morning and evening he knelt upon the ground and prayed. We knew not what he said, for his tongue was strange to us. He helped the men and women at their work, played with the children, and nursed the sick. He learned our language quickly, and then he began to tell us of a Great Teacher who had come to bless all people.

"'He held in his hand pieces of bark of a kind we knew not. They were fastened together and had writing on them that was not like the writing upon our lodges. These he held reverently, for he said it was "the writing sent by the Great Spirit to his children."

"'Day by day we gathered in the lodges or under the shade of the trees, and listened to the holy man as he sang sweet songs and taught them to us in our native tongue. He prayed and the sick were healed. He struck the ground, poured water upon it, and food came out of it for young and old.

"'We prayed to him, and then he became angry. "I am only a man," he said; "pray to the Great Spirit." We followed him wherever he went, and blessings came to us. Again and again he told us the story of the Great Teacher, and we drank eagerly of his words. The sick and the aged sent for him and said, "Tell it over again!" and when he told it they said, "Tell it again!"

"'One day when the people were assembled listening to his words, a little child sat beside him. Again he related the glory of the coming Great Chief, of the peace and joy that would dwell in our camps when the little children should know and love Him. As he looked upon the writing and sang and prayed, his lips quivered and tears flowed from his eyes. The little child by his side looked up into his face and then at the people, and whispered, "Apauakas!"

"'Then the people fell upon their faces and cried with one voice, "Apauakas! Apauakas!" As they rose they saw the white stranger on his knees and heard him say, "He has come! Christ has come!"

"As the aged chief Jacob related this to me, the people in the lodge clasped their hands together and sang a song about Apauakas, whom they called the Christ. When they had finished, Jacob took my hand and said, 'Young man, the Great Teacher has come; stay with us and you will see Him soon, for He dwells in our hearts and gives us peace.' I therefore stayed in the camp and looked daily for His coming, but I saw Him not.

"My heart was sad, and I prayed to the spirits of the prairie to help me. I walked, turning over in my thoughts all the wonderful things I had heard. I fell upon my face and groaned, 'Apauakas! Apauakas!' Brothers, my cry was answered: a bright light shone around me, and a voice from the overhanging clouds said gently, 'Arise! Apauakas has come. Call me no longer Apauakas, but Christ, for I shall aid and deliver you from all your foes!'

"I arose and sped towards the camp, and as the people saw me coming, they ran to meet me, shouting, 'He has found the Christ! The Christ has come!' I sang for joy, and the weeks fled as if they were but hours.

"One day the chief came to me and said, 'Brother, a messenger has come from the south bearing sad tidings. Sickness and death are in the camps of your people. Go, tell them of Apauakas the Great Teacher, who will relieve and bless them in their hours of woe.'

"I bade him farewell and hurried homeward. My heart sank within me as I came through the wood

near the camp and beheld the trees bearing the bodies
of my people whom I had left strong and well. I
bring a message of peace. Apauakas has come to
bless and heal His children. Chief, I have finished."

The eager eyes and haggard countenances of the
men who listened to the young man's story had been
strained and then relaxed as they followed the story
with absorbing interest to the end. A great silence fell
upon the lodge, and one by one the men arose and
went away to their own lodges. They spoke no word,
but pondered in silence over the strange things that
they had heard. Throughout the next day they
talked to each other by the lodge fires; the coming
of Apauakas was the burden of the stories told to the
women, and a deep, earnest longing took possession of
their hearts. At evening time they waited and
prayed, but He came not. Despair began once more
to be depicted on the faces of the people, and the signs
of a coming storm added fear to their misery. The
sky grew dark, the air heavy. As they waited in an
agony of spirit for the consummation of all their woes,
the storm broke, and as it increased in strength the
women prayed. One voice alone was heard above
the wild wailing of the wind, and the terror-stricken
inmates of the lodges listened as it sang, " Apauakas
is coming ! coming soon !"

At this the women stilled their whispered prayers
and waited, looking for the Teacher. The rain ceased
to beat upon the lodges, the clouds were swept
from the sky, the sun shone out in all its glory, and
the air seemed full of voices singing words of love
and tenderness.

They looked to where the young man knelt, and
saw that a smile of joy rested on his face as he gazed
up into the heavens. A strange feeling of awe made
them bow their heads. When they looked again they
saw he had fallen to the ground. They ran to him,
and as they raised him in their arms, gazing in pity
into his face, he murmured, "Apauakas has come!"
and closed his eyes.

A beautiful spot on the prairie is the honored resting-place of the gentle messenger of love; the Great
Teacher had come and taken him home. Health,
peace and comfort returned to the people, bringing
with them a better knowledge, a nobler life. The
stranger who now sits in the lodges and listens to the
stories told by the Indians will hear the young man's
name repeated with reverence as the prophet who led
his people to look for the coming of the Teacher, and
see eyes suffused with tears as they repeat,

"APAUAKAS HAS COME! THE CHRIST HAS COME!"

Forest, Lake and Prairie

TWENTY YEARS OF FRONTIER LIFE IN WESTERN CANADA, 1842-1862.

By JOHN McDOUGALL.

With 27 Full-Page Illustrations by J. E. Laughlin.

PRICE, $1.00.

Read the following comments:

"This is a true boy's book, and equals in stirring interest anything written by Kingston or Ballantyne. It ought to sell by the thousand."—Mrs. S. A. Curzon, in *Orillia Packet*.

"Possessed of an intimate acquaintance with all the varied aspects of frontier life, Mr. McDougall has produced a book that will delight the heart of every boy reader."—*Endeavor Herald*.

"There are many graphic descriptions of scenes in that vast fertile region in those early days when travelling was difficult and dangerous, but most fascinating to a youth of John McDougall's temperament and training. He lives those stirring times over again in his lively narrative, and relates his personal experiences with all the glow and vividness of an ardent, youthful hunter."— *Canadian Baptist*.

WILLIAM BRIGGS, Publisher, Toronto.

Canadian Savage Folk

The Native Tribes of Canada.

. . . BY . . .

JOHN MACLEAN, M.A., Ph.D.

AUTHOR OF 'THE INDIANS OF CANADA,' 'THE WARDEN OF THE PLAINS,' ETC.

In one volume, 642 pages, fully illustrated and handsomely bound.

PRICE, - - $2.50

CONTENTS: SOME QUEER FOLK—IN THE LODGES—CHURCH AND CAMP—NATIVE HEROES—NATIVE RELIGIONS, RACES AND LANGUAGES—ON THE TRAIL.

"There is no man in Canada, possibly anywhere, who has made a more careful, painstaking life-work in the study of the aboriginal races and all the writings extant relative to them, their traditions and history, than Dr. John Maclean. . . . While gleaning information from all the recognizedly authentic sources, Dr. Maclean, by his personal experience and individual knowledge, has added not only a vast amount of hitherto unpublished material, but has revivified and reset the old in the most attractive and readable form."—*The Week.*

"The whole ground is covered with a wealth of historic knowledge, while the style makes it as interesting as a romance. The author's familiarity with the subject, being for years a missionary in the far North-West, makes the work a thoroughly reliable treatise."—*Napanee Register.*

WILLIAM BRIGGS, Publisher, Toronto.